Roads and Parking Lots

Sophisticated Monkey

www.mcdaeth.com

ISBN 978-0-615-22368-1

The Meaning of My Nonexistence

Hippy dropped me at the parents' door, they came out blinking in the twilight – they were not expecting me. The Old Man stumbled onto the driveway, "I knew you'd be back, but not this goddamn fast." I'd only been gone a week after vowing never to return. I gave Hippy a shake and he slipped me a joint for later. It was the last free ride ever. There are still good people in the world. But not here.

I jumped out and awe-shucked my way into the house. They followed after. The Old Man said, "Well, where the hell ya been? Your mother thought you were dead." He looked at the Mom with more a command than a question, "Isn't that right?" They weren't sad just a little disappointed. "There are some leftovers," said the Mom trying to hold back the night with her apron. Christ, I was hungry, but more than that I needed sleep.

And sleep I did, almost the entire winter. I barely raised an eyelash except to find a drink. Even then I was exhausted, broken, done in. I leaned against fish houses on twenty feet of ice, didn't know how I got there, it didn't matter, I refused to go one step further, "I'm fine just where I'm at, you fuckers go on without me." My drinking buddies weren't doing much better than I, they could barely tilt their heads in any one direction for any length of time. They sat on their hands, mostly, with the heat on high and ACDC on low. They tried to save me, "Hey, Mick, ya stupid son of a bitch, yer gonna freeze yer ass off out there." I was done moving and there was no way they were getting out of the car to fetch me. They cranked 'em up and left me behind – even spit a little ice at me as they spun a circle around me and my fish house and got the hell out of there. It was some drunken riot.

I took in the stars with a twisted neck and slanted eyes. How could space be so empty with all that? I found the Big Dipper for the ten thousandth time and still looked forward to ten thousand one. I was alone in the cold empty winter – if you're gonna starve, starve in that, every bump in the sky looks almost edible.

I straightened up in the dark and navigated across the lake by the barking of the area dogs. That's how it goes up North; I knew the bark of everyone's dog. I kept the Aamodt's yipper to my right and the Riley's Setter to my left. The Thompson's big mutt howled in the background and the Henderson's Lab was my wandering dog star.

I crawled up the public landing in a snowmobile track. I kept my nose to it, it smelled of oil and gas. I felt the frozen patterns crackle and crunch under my feet – the human touch.

I stood at the top and looked back across the lake – it was flat black with a ring of blinking yard lights, further away than the stars. I left it at that. I wheeled around and took low, abbreviated steps quickly down the middle of the ice packed street and slid, on stiff knees and braced feet, toward the ditch. I kicked chunks of ice and they slid toward the ditch as well – there's a natural tendency.

I came to the railroad tracks; the same tracks that passed the back of the Old Man's mini-ranch. I followed them between frozen swamps and cut banks and wire bushes to our dead end road, then sliced through the thin gray trees – my trees – starving to death in a couple feet of snow. I pushed through and puffed forward to the other side and leaned against the last tree, still breathing. I never got tired of seeing my breath, I blew it through my fingers, down at my feet, watched it drift on the dead air, waved it with a hand. My shoes were packed tight with snow and ice – I was really there. In fact, I felt like I had always been there. When I was a kid I had these overwhelming feelings of my eternity. It didn't seem possible that I hadn't existed before and that I wouldn't exist after. I'd curl at the edge of my bed and concentrate with all my might – the meaning of my nonexistence. I couldn't do it.

I decided to spend the rest of the night in the cold under the last tree. I wouldn't start a fire either.

Hell is ice. The cold removes everything but it and you. In the cold, you lead with your ears, nose and toes. You are present and accounted for at all times. You know death. You see death. It's right over there beyond a break in the trees, frozen stiff. The cold also gives you the hint that it might not be so bad – to be entombed, preserved, forever in ice, through interstellar space. That's where the stars come in. Drift toward the brightest one and catch your breath.

Mission Texas

Spring arrived and the Old Man was a badger, "When are ya gonna get a goddamn job?" He was desperate for me to find work, nothing meaningful of course, just something to clock in and clock out of and get a slice. I had no interest in that. It was his fault really – his endless confrontation with life, work, happiness, me. I shrugged him off, used the mini-ranch like a freeway rest stop, piddled on the floor, missed the garbage can with an errant toss. He didn't give up, it wasn't in his nature, "You're eighteen now, if you're gonna live under my roof, ya gotta get a job and pay some rent." It was always his roof never our roof; Big Sister, Little Sister, the Mom and I were to be arranged according to his satisfaction.

The Old Man had row upon row of buttons I could punch. I found them all the hard way through the bobbing and weaving years, my unknown purpose vs. his Jack Dempsey. My bloody knuckles itched with the desire to punch every one of them, lights out for the Old Man, the big revenge for the bitter past. I rolled it around in my head for years and years where it was such a shivering pleasure to watch him toss on the rocks. But these days he could no longer stretch to his full six-feet-four-inch lanky frame – even though he didn't know it yet – the demon inside him was a dead weight, it pulled him low to the ground, upset his center of gravity. Despite everything, I felt sorry for him so I put him off instead, "Yeah, well, we'll talk about it later." He didn't like being brushed aside – he jumped up out of his seat and fell over in a mad rush at my shadow. I was already half way to the door when he yelled from his knees, "At least feed the goddamn horses and shovel the corral."

"No thanks."

"You cocky son of a bitch! I'll throttle you!"

On instinct, I made ready to run for it – let the Old Man cool in the shade of the Mom's apron for a few hours, let the demon put on a few more pounds, maybe. I threw a little fire retardant over my shoulder, "Don't worry, I'll get it done." I pawed the door open and was nearly through when the phone rang. I held my position with the door half cocked just in case it was for me: an invitation, a point B at which to arrive and circle the parking lot. The dog sniffed at my feet, the cats went in and out, the Mom called me back, "Grandpa's on the phone."

I put it to my ear, "Hey Gramps."

"Hey kid. Listen, we just bought a place in Texas and we need some help with the move, what're ya doing next week?"

"Nothing that can't wait I suppose."

"We'll give you a few hundred for helping us out how's that suit ya?"

"You don't have to do that."

"See ya next week."

I hung up the phone and headed for the door, the Old Man intervened, "Well, how much is he paying you?"

"He didn't say."

"Well, he's got to pay you something, goddamn it, I could've used you this summer for baling hay."

"Wait a second, he did mention something about giving me a few hundred bucks."

"What!? You're gonna take money from your own grandfather and after he gave you a car and everything! Christ, how ungrateful are you?"

As usual the Old Man wanted it both ways. Whatever side I was on, he was on the other and if I switched so would he. He opposed me from every angle; when I was sad he tried to make me happy, when I was happy he tried to make me sad. I learned to remain neutral on all fronts – a blank slate – I fought my battles on the inside at absolute zero. I didn't move a muscle even as others died: cousins off bridges, uncles in rollovers, pets that had roamed around with me for years and years. The only real thing to talk to and explore with was this wagging thing, this howling mess full of ticks so fat they'd fall to the ground blood bloated. I'd kick them to the concrete slab, drop a brick and measure the splatters – that's how I got it out.

The following week I headed for the grandparent's place down south in Mankato. I took the same route the parents used Christmas and Easter or to drop us off for a few weeks every summer before heading out West somewhere without us. It was great. In the early days, the cousins would wait for us on the front steps. They were just as scrawny as us – we'd instantly get into it – chase each other in circles – on bare feet – over the petrified grass – down the dark ravines – water balloon fights – flash lighting cars after dark.

One muggy evening I was out with a cousin a couple years younger. We stood at the edge of the street and I directed him when and where to throw our collection of sticks and stones: passing cars, street lights, tree trunks, front doors. A girl with long blonde hair rode past on a banana seat popping wheelies in the street. Impressive, I thought. "Throw a stick at her, Young Cousin," I said. It was a good toss – hit her right on the thigh. She jumped off that banana seat in such a way that it made me hesitate, suddenly I knew why; the girl was a guy, way bigger than either of us and he was closing in fast. Young Cousin was quick that night – we stretched side by side while Long Blonde Dude ate up the distance between us then reached out for me. I could feel his fingernails ready to dig in. I panicked, grabbed Young Cousin by the collar and pulled him down behind me, clipping Long Blonde Dude at the knees. He took a header into the petrified grass. I jumped over the lip of the ravine into the dark. Safe.

After some minutes holding my breath, I peered over the lip but I couldn't make anything out. I crept onto the petrified grass and bent through the shadows to the edge of the backyard light. Grandma was at the backdoor with Young Cousin, perfectly fine. I stepped out of the shadows toward the door. Then I saw, in my periphery, out of another shadow, Long Blonde Dude sprinting to cut me off and give me what I had coming. I took off running for Grandma. She never looked so good. She held the door open and I slipped through just out of reach of Long Blonde Dude again. He was furious, told Grandma the story of the stick being thrown. Young Cousin and I held fast to our denials and we won the night. I apologized to Young Cousin later that evening, "I swear I thought he was a girl."

As the years rolled on, the circles filled in as the cousins were tied up in teenage pregnancies and fast food work and their un-employed, alcoholic dad. He was Grandma's brother and a hard alcohol alcoholic. Gramps said that made all the difference. The cheap booze pulled him apart. He seeped like me. He was a low pressure cloudy day – a bricklayer who could no longer perform in the appropriate position – people were tired of loaning him money to buy back the cement mixer. He spent his last days living with his mom – great grandma Reed. He sat in a grease track on a cream colored recliner with an ashtray close at hand – the kind that stood on a hollow leg with a button to trigger a trap door to dump the butts and ash into a little tin pail hanging down the center. He pulled it out and dumped it twice a day, sunup and sundown. I couldn't help but tear up whenever I got near him. He looked like the future, so utterly used up.

The neighborhood was crammed with aunts and uncles and cousins in various states of bloom and decay. Every other house contained a relative of some sort, mostly from the Mom's side. I was free to wander all the way to a little shopping mall with a Walgreens and a Sears and a tiny set of ever changing retail satellites. Right next to Sears there was a dead end hall that held a little arcade, pinball machines etc. I hung out there with the cousins or down in Gramps' basement bar with its dark paneling, blue smoke, buzzing and blinking neon beer signs, wraparound leather couch and big TV piping in eleven channels from the Twin Cities.

Cable! I nailed myself to the wraparound and stuffed my face with all the latest sugar treats and caught up on popular culture on laugh tracks and in syndication. Every commercial break found me scampering up the stairs to see if Gramps needed a beer. "Here ya go Gramps." He paid very well. He dug into his bottomless pocket of loose change and dished it out, "Let's see here, tell ya what, this time I'm gonna give you all the dimes." I added them in my head as I added them to my pocket, then stood by for my sip of beer because out of each beer I got a sip – it was a tradition dating way back to my perilous threes. Eighteen bottles a day give or take – I pulled a little more out of each sip. Just like Gramps I was a happy drunk, we'd go fishing for bullheads or just sit on the concrete slab and laugh about something he said or a face he made or my goofy voice. It was the only time I could get a full breath. I'd cling to him. I'd even ride-along-with on his bar tours through North Mankato, sat alone in the car while he bellied up to the bar for a couple hours then returned with a six pack, just enough to get us home, a mile or so, depending on the curve of the earth...

As I pulled up the driveway, Gramps was already loading-up a 1940-something six ton grain truck he'd driven off a farm the day before. Forty years hauling corn, now it held Grandma's sewing machine and nine thousand other items newspaper-wrapped and cardboard-boxed. The back of the six ton stood over six feet off the ground. Gramps used a stepladder to climb up in and turnaround and reach down for the cardboard boxes that Grandma, with crooked glasses that matched her crooked frown, lifted up to him on wobbly toes. She was ahead of her time – a career girl, office managed the local radio station – never missed a Sunday service at Immanuel Lutheran church and neither did the kids. At home she handled the checkbook and savings and everything else that was important while Gramps took forty-five sips an hour from a returnable case of North Star beer. He kept ten cases on hand in the basement lined up opposite the washer and dryer. He shuffled through them as a plain matter of fact. It was no secret that he loved his beer and Camels. He'd sit at the kitchen table, in an ash blue ensemble, flicking a well-oiled lighter or tipping a cold bottle with icy greased fingers.

This move to Texas was Gramps' first push in over thirty years and Grandma was doing her best to play the agreeable wife. He'd caught her by surprise when they were on a two week vacation in South Texas. His brother, Jack, was already planted there six months out of the year – semi-retired in a trailer park – with sun baked bones and an armadillo shell. Right next door, there was a brick rambler for sale by owner. It sat on four weedy acres. Gramps made an offer while Grandma was out shopping and, by the time she returned, he had gathered too much momentum – already put down the earnest money. He howled and moaned when Grandma told him to get it back, "What kind of old fool are you?" He stomped around his brother's trailer like a two year old and threatened to run away and join the circus if he didn't get his way. She wasn't impressed. He pulled out the big gun – he'd even give up beer if that's what it took and only drank six cans that day to show he was serious. He hadn't left Minnesota in sixty years, and now he didn't want to go back, not ever. Almost sober, he rolled over the top of her and she was bitter, and would be for years, but for now she still had nine thousand items to go and she hadn't even gotten to the attic, kitchen, or the crap tacked to the walls and, by god, she was determined to wrap every last hunk of bric-a-brac. "You boys go on ahead, I've still got things to do."

I helped Gramps round off the load and tie down the tarp. It was still early afternoon and Gramps wanted to go fishing one last time, so we dug some worms in the blue earth garden and headed to the lake in his red El Camino. We were after bullheads and sunnies with little bobbers, tiny hooks and baby sinkers. In my younger days I man-handled the bullheads, ripped out the hook with a vengeance and slam dunked them in the bucket. I didn't know they had stingers and was never stung. But one day, when I saw Gramps nursing a bloody finger and found out the cause, I could no longer get a grip on them. From then on, when I snagged one, I'd flip it on shore and hold it down with a shoe while I pried out the hook with a pair of pliers. Then, I'd kick it toward the bucket and let Gramps take it from there.

We brought home fifteen bullheads and six sunnies. I scraped the scales off the sunnies by going against the grain with a spoon, leaving thousands of tiny fingernails on Sunday's paper. I slit open the belly with a whetstone knife and scooped it clean with the spoon, then cut off the head with a single stroke of the knife. What remained was rinsed under the faucet, then dropped in a pan of salt water and moved to the refrigerator. Gramps took care of the bullheads with a little knife slice around the throat, then with the pliers he clipped in the slice and stripped off the skin down to the tail. A few hours later, Grandma battered up some flour and corn-meal, dropped a dab of Crisco in a frying pan, turned on the natural gas burner and they made their last fishy move with a dip, roll, and drop into the hot grease courtesy of Grandma's seasoned limbs. The sizzling smell brought me up from the basement bar, where I took a bite and got a fishbone stuck in my throat. It was not enough to cut off the air or anything, just a wedged piece of cartilage that I couldn't get down or cough up. Grandma suggested, "Chew some bread and wash it down with a glass of water. That might push it through." I gummed up half a loaf, tongue and grooved each bite into pasty balls and rolled them down the back of my throat. It didn't work, nothing worked. Grandma gave up first, "Well, you will just have to wait for the bone to dissolve."

I spent the night in the basement, sipping a North Star, stuck to the wraparound in front of the cable, no Big Dipper in sight. Grandma shook me loose at four in the morning – my eyes still staring at the fuzzy box – my mind still set to the bone in my throat. It was the last thing I remembered and first thing I thought of. It nagged me all the way up the stairs and beyond the kitchen table, where Gramps was just cracking his first beer after a plate of bacon and eggs, "Make a sandwich, we gotta get on the road."

We hooked the aluminum fishing boat to the back of the red El Camino. I was to drive that while Gramps led with the six ton and his cooler of beer. He got lost on the way out of town – went straight down Adams street and found the dead end – couldn't back-it back out – or read the mirrors – the gear box was tricky – the load was too heavy – the street was too narrow. He sucked down a few more beers to calm his nerves and made it out of there on the thirty-fifth try, then took highway 14 westbound. We were supposed to go east.

I didn't notice at first, my job was to follow, but I'm good with funny feelings. As we crawled along, the sun rose. I kept staring at my shadow running in front between the lines, squirreling the landscape, flashing to and fro on a cornering road. Suddenly, a billboard: Visit the Corn Palace in Mitchell, South Dakota! "Goddamn!" I flashed my headlights at Gramps but he just kept on going – double clutched to his top end of forty-five miles per hour. I had to drive into oncoming traffic to flag him down. The red El Camino had plenty of motor, but the boat trailer bounced and fishtailed at fifty so I could barely get around him – we were stuck with each other. I got him to the side of the road with desperate gestures and schizophrenic features. He down-shifted to a stalled motor. I parked behind, got out, ran up along side and let him off easy, "Shouldn't we be going east toward Owatonna?"

"Yup."

"We're heading west toward South Dakota."

He cracked his ninth beer and squinted at his map, "I can't read this damn thing." He handed it down to me from his six ton cab, "See what you can make of this."

I knew without looking, "Turn around and head east toward Owatonna then take I-35 south for the next fifteen hundred miles." I was a map-smith as a kid. On lonely icebound nights I'd plot my escape routes on a Rand McNally – different pens – different inks – different paths – all the way to the setting sun. I'd follow rivers as faint blue lines easily lost in the hub-bub of getting somewhere, seeing something: an evergreen tree, a picnic bench, a hook up, a look-over, a scavenging rodent.

We passed back through Mankato around noon, already seven hours on the road. I banged on the wheel and felt like going back to the house and telling Grandma, but then I caught Gramps making a face in the driver's side mirror as he worked through beer number twelve – double figures – in his prime – safely beyond sober. I tucked behind his tailgate and stayed the course on his weaving road.

Gramps stopped to fill up in Waseca. The six ton managed only four to six miles per gallon depending on the direction of the wind and the size of the hill. There were two gas tanks installed and Gramps could toggle between them with a little switch on the dash. They took forever to fill, so I pulled along the edge and went in for anything that might shake loose the bone in my throat.

The gas station was old time oily. They still fixed cars and sold tires. I bought a stale Snickers, a bag of Old Dutch potato chips and a

Mello Yello from the wife of the head mechanic. She handed me my change. Her hands were stained from hand jobs – changing the oil and filter, gapping the plugs. Head Mechanic sat just inside the open-door garage whittling a carburetor. Gramps called him out with the ding-ding of the trigger line bell. Head Mechanic leaned against the six ton and while the gas pump rang like a slot machine he yucked it up with Gramps, laughed about some thing, shook his head over the future, wiped his hands on a wiped out rag. It was a fuzzy gray June day and the passing cars echoed between the pumps with a lullaby of gloom and doom.

Once Gramps got off the road anything could happen, he was just as likely to go back the way he came, no instinct whatsoever, couldn't read the signs, double guessed in the wrong direction every time. I'd scream myself hoarse from the dirty background, "A RIGHT! TAKE A RIGHT! NOW!" It was maddening to see him cruise past the arrow pointing south and mix himself in the northbound traffic. I'd have to bounce him to the side and get him turned around. He wouldn't let me lead. As long as I was in the side mirrors, at least we were lost together.

We nosed east toward Owatonna. Gramps was driving on beer number fifteen. The morning's dead end chug-a-lug meant it would be a short road. We were already entering the dark side of the hour when he leaned his head forward and drove out of the corners of his eyes, while all manner of nastiness poured out of his chest. I could see him in his side mirrors, raging against the white lines like they were lightning strikes or stabs to his heart. It was bad. I kept pushing him forward.

I rode along in the red El Camino and wondered if we would ever get there on this long, beautiful, meaningless road with floating hawks and swooping crows. A bluebird sits on a post in a cloud shadow while the street milling ants are getting the rubout from the red El Camino and distant winged cousins splatter the windshield.

Oh Gramps, just a few more miles, just a few more miles, follow your nose – German, red, sausage on a face full of purple pimples and pores as wide as iron ore pits scattered all the way to your receding hairline. A tiny dribble of tear tucked and rolled down my cheek. I quickly brushed it away and bounced off the dashboard, "Get a hold of yourself Mick, there's no time for this. Gramps has been worse off – all the times he crashed his truck into the side of the house – or the early years spent so wasted he beat the wife before Grandma, and then Grandma."

On the road Gramps was a worrywart. A crackerjack mechanic, he had a skeletal view of the world and all the shit that can break just trying to get around. He preferred his beer on the concrete slab, staying put, maybe cracking a walnut shell, puffing a Camel, sipping the can – that was it. I knew, deep down below the bone in my throat, I knew, it was up to me to get us to the Rio Grande. I would lead from the rear if I had to, but I would get us there because I would do anything for that crazy, wonderful, horrible alcoholic.

Just west of Owatonna, I-35 bled into the picture and Gramps fell right onto the southbound ramp, things were looking up. I was hoping that on the freeway he would open up the throttle and get it up to sixty. Instead, he hugged the right lane and dropped it to forty. The sky was so wide open he'd get lost in it and pull his foot off the gas. The leftward swerving trucks and cars blared their horns and screamed on by, the entire world was dissatisfied with our progress.

It took most of the day to clear the Minnesota border and find Iowa much the same, barely a gap in the cornfields. I had plenty of time to watch it grow, count telephone poles, follow the droopy power lines, search the weedy ditch for wishful bags of money, dream about the great big black wide open nothing that lay ahead. What is there to do? When there's nothing to do but wait for nuclear annihilation.

I pulled Gramps to the side with powder puffed headlights and forced a bologna and cheese sandwich down his gullet. He tottered in the six ton while I sat on the other side of the cooler and poured him a coffee from the thermos and told him to drink, drink drink, flat black, no sugar. "Now let's take a walk down that path by the road and stretch our legs a little." He bitched and moaned while I dashed around and helped him out of the six ton and dragged him back and forth along a cornfield. Happy Gramps was somewhere else, back home perhaps, hosing down the concrete slab, it didn't matter now, this was mission Texas all the way.

I willed Gramps down the highway with a furrowed brow while the bone in my throat dug deeper and deeper and I was a prisoner to it all. Forty miles an hour or less down the bowel of America, and it is – you can smell the pesticides on the dusty breeze, the pig shit, cow shit – and if you put an ear to the ground you can hear the gurgle of millions of steel straws sucking up the Ogallala Aquifer. This is where the infinite dreams meet the finite world and it all gets washed into the Mississippi and pushed out into the Gulf.

By six in the evening Gramps had had enough. His milky red eyes said it all, his 16 hour thirty-six beer day was over. I got him to the side by tooting the horn and flashing the headlights as usual. "There's a motel at the next exit let's take it."

"Huh? Wha?"

"Stay behind me."

I ran to the red El Camino, jacked it around him, puttered it up to forty and left him in the dust. I yelled at the rearview mirror, "goddamn it anyway!" took it down to twenty-five and bumped the shoulder until finally Gramps was back in view. I took the next exit and he managed to follow me to a motel/restaurant. We were still north of Des Moines. I got us a room with twin beds and an anchored-down television. I carried him to the restaurant and ordered him a charred steak and baked potato. Gramps packed it away, somehow, while I sipped a bowl of cracker-less tomato soup.

I stayed up late with the bone in my throat and the slow motion white lines in my head and by the time I conked out, Gramps was up and at it with his first smoke of the day by the side of the bed in boxers and socks, "Get up kid we gotta hit the road." I opened my eyes and swallowed the dust mites – the bone was still there. This bone, this bone, this goddamn motherfucking bone. I pinned my eyes against it – pressed my lips against it – pinched my nose against it – put all thought against it. It held fast in the record heat through Missouri, Kansas, Oklahoma, Texas while the driver's side of my face and arm burned up. The rising sun was a bitch – I was a two sided man, devil red and white toast. The heat was too much for most. The road was an end unto itself – vehicles fell to the side with blown retreads, leaky hoses, squeaky belts, out of gas – grimy Americans trying to make it on their own in a land of roads and parking lots.

Early morning Gramps was full of blood and spit and eager to get started on the first beer of the day. We gassed up at a truck stop (Gramps refilled his cooler), crawled back onto I-35 south and plodded along. I thought, better the wobbly Gramps than the sober Old Man. I told the boys up North, "See you fuckers in ten days tops and we'll have the summer to end all summers." It was agreed – there would be no limit. I could see now that ten days would not suffice – we'd be lucky to get to the Rio Grande in a week at this pace then to unload and situate, knowing that Gramps would park himself on the concrete slab and not lift a finger except to fill the hole.

We drove along, the sun reared its ugly head and by ten in the morning it was 100 degrees and no air-conditioning in the red El Camino. I kept the windows cranked down and got wind blasted by passing trucks, cars and busses. There were dust clouds to the horizon, that was as far into the future as we could go.

Where was that rainy summer of my youth when there was an explosion of salamanders? They were everywhere, after dark, black with yellow speckles, prowling the lawn. We collected them in buckets. Who would fill theirs first? Who would get the most? The biggest? The smallest? The fastest? We raced them under the yard light, tried to make them fight each other on the gravel driveway, but they were only interested in waddling along. We dragged our buckets around with us, then, spotted some fireflies so dashed off to catch and put them in a mayonnaise jar where they would be dead by morning, "Ah, we forgot to poke some holes."

We left our buckets of salamanders, in the tall weeds still half full, and forgot about them. We stumbled over the buckets a week later while searching for the tiniest frog in the entire universe. There was a ten inch layer of dried salamanders in each bucket – shriveled up bodies, shrunken heads, flies crawling in and out of their gaping mouths. We flipped the buckets over, kicked the sides and the salamanders came out in clumps. The smell drove us away, but we returned with sticks and poked at the clumps for a while. There were no survivors. Then it was back to our epic search for the tiniest frog in the universe – God help him if we find him...

The afternoon rolled and we rolled and the highway rolled. Then, the forced feedings and cups of coffee and afternoon staggers I put Gramps through to get a few more miles before he was closed for the day. It seemed endless.

In the white hot early evening we pulled off for another motel/restaurant and, while Gramps snoozed in the twin bed, I wandered down to the soda machine, selected an Orange Crush and filled the bucket with ice hoping to get a glimpse of some sweet vacationing girls come for their Orange Crush and bucket of ice. And they came, arriving on flip flops and ravishing in tube tops and short shorts and mood rings and painted toenails. I looked at the one who looked away and didn't see the one who didn't and, anyway, I was caught up with the bone in my throat and my shallow breath. I went back to the room and the anchored-down television, poured some acid on the bone and tried to get some sleep before we were back at it.

We hit every population center at peak rush hour when zero to five was the norm and forty seemed like star cruising. Kansas City was like that and worse. One hundred fifteen degrees and the asphalt buckling under the weight of it all and great cavernous potholes opening spontaneously under axles and the traffic swerving and breaking down and folks walking along or just standing there on the side of the road helpless in the boiling day – dehydrated and dirty and hacking up their two pack habit and you thanked God you weren't one of them, you were close and you knew it, but still you gave them a wide berth – poverty is contagious.

In between the traffic jams there were the weigh stations and Gramps had to ride the scale at every one. He always stopped the front-end just off the scale and would have to find reverse and grind it backwards a few feet, but then be off the mark the other way and the weigh station employees would laugh and get irritated when he did it again! The drivers of the big sixteen wheelers from Gramps' backside pulled at their foghorns and swished their airbrakes and generally looked like they would murder him if he missed his next attempt – which he did. They didn't know that Gramps was an ace under the hood and could tear down, fix and reassemble the greatest diesels in the world in record time, so poor Gramps was the fool of the weigh station.

Every night the anchored-down television fed us tales of the heat wave – the death toll – the victims. The sad sweaty survivors stood on the porch, in the doorway, on the dirt lawn, holding a wrinkled photo of the dearly departed. I imagined myself standing there, holding a picture of Gramps because he was dead in Oklahoma by the side of the road, in a dust bowl, under a great big iron grasshopper. Then the anchored-down television turned to sports and a feel-good story and I went back to the bone in my throat and Gramps lived on.

Texas at last and its dusty Cadillacs, oversized cowboy hats and torched sunsets. One hundred-twenty degrees in the shade, and there wasn't any anyway and either way Gramps kept on drinking and driving and weighing in and filling up and falling down.

The freeway exits were full of vagabond bums, some as young as I. Could it be that I was one of the lucky ones? It didn't seem possible, but there they were staggering down the line. I took a deep breath and passed out cans of soda and bags of chips in truck stop parking lots to the orphans of the road and would have done more if I'd had more money or a gun to get more money – I was that pissed off about it – but then I was back in the red El Camino nursing Gramps along and I forgot all about them.

Through the magnificent vastness of horrible Texas we dueled dust storms and the yellow rose and lost ourselves outside of San Antonio. We circled it three times – Gramps kept missing the exit – so very goddamn hot. On turn number three the traffic came to a sudden standstill. Gramps was digging in the cooler and when he finally looked up, it was right there in front of him. He had to stomp on the brake pedal with all his weight to avoid the rear-end. He skidded within a couple of inches. I was just as lucky. I was tucked in a little too close to his mud flaps, daydreaming about something. I slid into the back of the six ton and coughed up the bone in my throat – hallelujah! – it landed on the dash and began to sizzle – it was that goddamn hot. The bone burned black into the dash leaving a permanent mark.

Gramps staggered to the side and got out to inspect. The red El Camino was a little bumped and scratched, but the front brake lines on the six ton were blown out so Gramps had to ride the rear brakes the rest of the way. To stay on the safe side, he took it down to fifteen miles per hour. The armadillos crossed in front of us at their leisure. They mocked us with their armored shells. I'd get fed up, pull around Gramps, ram on ahead, pull off, find some overhang and eventually Gramps would come creeping down the road, give me a wave and a face and we'd begin again.

After eleven days and ten nights on the road we arrived at the brick rambler. Gramps took a long nap, but I wanted to see the river so I kept on going. Ah, to be out from the back of that corn truck, the taillights pressed to my head, the dirty mud flaps, side view mirror Gramps!

I landed at Peppy's on the River – a real live shit hole. It was nearly sunset and still ridiculously hot and there were jet skis on the Rio Grande going wide open back and forth in front of a dusty landing. The end of the road was a Tex-Mex Tiki hut – outdoors only except for the toilet. You ate your barbecue and drank your beer on a picnic bench or a barstool and took in the sunburnt dancing in the dirt in front a double stack of cracked speakers, too far gone to notice the new blisters. It was business as usual and not much of a mystery who would get fucked before daybreak. Everyone wore their potential on their sleeves, any old snake bite would bring them down.

They paired off at random. They bounced off each other and fell in the dirt. True love was born when some drunk redneck extended a hand downward to help some drunk senorita off the ground. It was the nicest thing anyone had ever done for her. Such a gentleman. Quite unlike the pendejos from her neighborhood. She, of course, needed a shoulder to lean on. The best he could offer was another round and she accepted because you take the bad with the good. Would this be her high and her low – what with getting tipsy and him fucking her in the tall weeds by the river? And when he was through she helped him up and he leaned on her to the parking lot.

As for me, I spent the night at the bar next to a man who was smiling and giggling to himself in that fucked-up sort-of-way drunks get when they're about to turn the motor over one last time. He had sad baggy eyes and bony fingers that held a cigarette – he had two behind the ear and a pack in his front shirt pocket. Together they were one long cigarette chain, the burnt down lit the next one in line and so on, while he was busy getting the facts straight for a demonstration, a justification, a series of lights, a load of bricks, an assembly line, a new born something. I caught his eye because I was the next stool over. He said, "Reagan's gonna fuck it up, man. Know what I mean?"

"Yeah, not really."

"A fucking actor president? That's it, my friend, words don't mean shit, man, words don't mean shit."

"Yeah."

"Stay off the freeway, punk, its not fucking free."

"Yeah?"

"It murders the soul, all that concrete so out of proportion says you are now a number. It reduces the world to two points, where you start and where you end. That's not traveling that's fascism! Fucking Nazis invented the freeway, look it up man, don't be a fucking pawn."

Here was an interesting man, a skunk drunk philosopher of the Rio Grande. The jet skis buzzed on the river like giant mosquitoes, the rock 'n' roll pumped up and down through the cracked speakers, the sunburnt danced their lives away. He asked, "Did you know that the freeways run over and through our vital and sacred lands?"

"Yeah, no."

"Of course you didn't. They don't talk about that sorta shit. The freeways were built to annihilate the poor and the small town. Words don't mean shit, man, words don't mean shit." He was near the end of another link, he rotated one in from the ear and continued, "You're as helpless as a lamb, my friend, when it comes to the future and you always will be so get used to it."

"Yeah."

"Words don't mean shit, man, words don't mean shit."

Life cuts corners wherever it can. Some asshole living it up out in the parking lot screamed, "Whaa-hOOOoooo!" and sent a leaded kiss through the sway-backed crowd. It was some magic bullet, it bobbed and weaved and bounced off the ground and somehow missed everyone but the man at the bar. He was smacked in the head – a clean hit – a steel jacket – a sudden crack – a pregnant pause – a widespread panic – everyone scattered to parts unknown – I drove back to the brick rambler and hid behind the drapes. Two weeks behind the drapes – I can't fill in the blanks.

Speed Freak

He lived across the dirt road, a speed freak, working for the border authorities checking Ag trucks coming across the border from Mexico. A bouncy little guy, maybe twenty-five, a foot tapper, a knuckle cracker, with a patch of red hair and ten thousand freckles just trying to keep up. He wandered over to the brick rambler and asked the only important question, "So where ya from?" (tap tap tap crack crack crack)

"Minnesota."

"Me too! St. Peter!" (tap tap tap crack crack crack).

"Gramps lives in Mankato. I live a lot further north."

"Mankato! So we're neighbors up there too."

Speed Freak volunteered to be my tour guide of northern Mexico – actually he insisted, "No problem, I mean, we're neighbors and we're both from Minnesota. You can always trust someone from Minnesota." We tapped and cracked our way across the border. I soon discovered that he was looking for someone, his speed dealer, a man named José. We circled the town square, "Anybody seen José?" Everybody had seen José and they directed our path down alleys, past carts, through shops. We were as little as five minutes behind to as much as two days, depending on the José. Speed Freak sensed my frustration, "Hey, Mick, something will shake loose, we'll find José yet. Come on, I'll buy you something to eat." He said "we" like I was part of the deal.

He left me next to the fountain in the town square with a roasted chicken, a coke and a couple napkins. I soon had a ring of teeth and eyes. I felt the need to share my roasted chicken with them, but there were no takers. I lost my appetite.

I walked up and down the narrow broken down lanes with a wagging tail of four to eight year olds – all of them talking at once. It made me smile. I knew what they were talking about. Down the street came beautiful senoritas so tiny and delicate and shy and wonderful. I fell in love every couple steps. A raging love, a burning love, the last icicle dropped from my heart and nailed my foot to the Mexican dirt.

I wanted to kill all the fat middle-aged gringo tourists I saw haggling with the Mexicans over blankets, hats, pottery – shaking them down with fat fuckin' frowns. Pulling the kind of shit they wouldn't dream of back home at Kmart or Sears.

"Hey, I'm doing you a favor here."

"English, sweetheart, can you speak English?"

"I'll give you five dollars for it and not a penny more."

"A dollar down here can go a goddamn mile."

"These peasants will steal you blind if you let them."

I hated them. I wanted to sweep the streets clear of them, take their money and let the wind decide where it should go. I wanted to dress the senoritas in gold, embrace them all, hold them up to the light and see what I could see. I wanted to be one of them – I was one of them. In a deep breath, I felt something pure, earthy, true, walking their streets with them. But then I caught my sad pale reflection in a window with a long jaggedy diagonal crack and just like that, the feeling was gone. My breath returned to its constricted norm. I returned to the other side of the world, alone with my ridiculous thoughts, sad, bitter, lonely. I couldn't even love myself for very long let alone anyone else. I parked my ass back at the fountain. The chicken and coke were gone, even the napkins. I sat like a lump and took it all in like a Hollywood movie: [Final Scene: Speed Freak arrives with a bundle of pills – he says to Mick] "Let's get some tequila." [Mick nods his head and says] "Yes." [The wind kicks up a dust devil near the fountain and it blows on down the dusty street – the sun is merely a blink on the horizon. The teeth and eyes gather 'round and sing "La Cucaracha" – Mick makes eyes with the prettiest senorita in the town square. The camera pulls back slowly – there's a swell of violins – all is well – the revolution will have to wait.]

Speed Freak tapped and cracked his way out of his job and tapped and cracked through his money. In a matter of days he was all the way down the hill. I winced in anticipation of the impending crash – a car going too fast, can't make the corner, a car coming the other way, the screeching tires that reach into infinity, you can't lift your head 'til its over, then you can't look away.

Speed Freak and I were no longer speaking, though I did try to talk him out of taking so much speed.

"Listen, Speed Freak, what good has taking all that speed done for you?"

He wouldn't be deterred, "Are you kidding? I once won a corn shucking contest back in St. Peter. And I own the record for most canned corn at the Jolly Green Giant processing plant."

He was down to his last minutes. He kept checking to see if his car would start. He never went anywhere he'd just shut it off, go back in his hut and do it again ten minutes later. He ran down the battery, went on checking until there was no longer a click from the starter and the dome light was dead. He moved to the next obsession – chopping down the tall weeds that were everywhere with an ancient scythe. One sun blasted August day he stormed across the

27

street and swung it around in Gramps' front yard. A mere five minutes later, ringing wet, he sought payment with a rat-tat-tat-tat on the front door. I cracked the blind on a side window. He looked like the grim reaper. I didn't answer. I let him hammer away – desperate – grinding his teeth – locked in his head – having a conversation with the shadows.

I wanted to go home. Hell isn't ice. Hell is fire. The burning sun took me down and left me there, a teenage orphan. I didn't know the siesta system so I marched right on through the middle of the day, just me and the roadrunners and the lizards and the dead orange grove and the migrant path that ran up from the river. I stayed up late and counted the migrants as they passed. It was a one way street, nothing but oncoming traffic.

I begged Gramps, "Come on, lets go lets go lets go!"

"We can't head back until I get the new brakes for the six ton."

I patrolled the dirt road looking out for the truck that would deliver me from Hell. Day after day – nothing – no parts arrived. I demanded that Gramps get them on the blower and find out what the hold up was. It turned out that the parts had been returned to the parts depot because Gramps had given them the wrong address in the late afternoon of his eighteenth beer. Up and down I screamed and hollered. I was missing the whole damn summer. All my mates were high on ditch weed, mini tornadoes, giant mosquitoes, beer parties, and the pretty suburban girls who rode up for long weekends with their parents to one of the many lakeside parking lots that dotted the North country. Not to mention the small-town girls who spent the summer cleaning their cabins, waitressing their meals and screwing us. I was sick and tired of Speed Freak rapping on the door. It went off at the top of every hour, In-a-Gadda-Da-Vida played backwards with rubber band knuckles on the crappy solid core. No deadbolt, just a twisty lock on the door knob – no way it was gonna hold up forever. Eventually I had to let him in. He stayed for three days. Said they were after him – we never found out who. He drank up all the beer. That's when Gramps had had enough so he took out his 16 gauge side by side and pointed the way past the mailbox.

The end of each squint-eyed day found me loaded down with Gramps' Lone Star returnables. He drank during the day and I drank at night. It was a peaceful arrangement as long as I kept the fridge well-stocked. He left tens and twenties on the kitchen counter and I wore a migrant path to the beer aisle.

Gramps kept me in South Texas almost the entire summer. It took him nearly a month after the parts arrived to fix the six ton. He didn't want to get back on that fucking road. "To hell with the other nine thousand items!" he screamed from his soul. He loved the breeze that blew in from the Gulf every evening. We sat on the concrete slab, just like old times for him, but not quite, and never again the same for me. I was antsy, I had to get moving and keep moving and Gramps keeping me there at the end of his life was too much to bear. I wish now that I had listened a little closer to his stories.

The Rice Plant

Autumn was turning and I was anxious to get away from the mini-ranch, but I had no money for that, so I scanned the want ads for any damn thing that would do and found it at the local wild rice plant. The job was to help wherever help was needed – according to the higher ups – they controlled the when, where and how. I was a thing they put in action. I was to have no will of my own nor concern for anything but the task handed down – can do, will do, for $5.40 an hour. "Hey, Mick, a truck just came in with a load of loose rice, get your ass up in there and shovel it clean." You gotta learn it from the bottom up and if you remain on the bottom, well then, it's your fault, they gave you a chance. "Hey, Mick, hold on to that shovel, you're gonna need it to help Stan top-off the front-end loader and don't forget to meet him out back on the tarps with a rake 'cause we'll need you to spread every dump flat. Chop-chop we don't have all day."

About a week into the grind I was moved to the nightshift and given a nickel more an hour for the inconvenience. It wasn't so bad, the higher ups were all tucked away in bed while I stood on the foggy ground and leaned against the rake and followed the sounds of owl and prey somewhere in the sticky black trees, skating the drizzling sky over the plastic tarp field. Me thinking, what is it that's out there that I can't see? I was buried above ground in sneakers and flannel and a twitchy eyelash. I had barely a rough outline to go by except the black tree tips stabbing the gray gray gray – that was clear enough.

A pothead friend of mine arrived one night with his big bag of weed. I was drinking a can of Mello Yello in the break room when he arrived for his first night of work, thirty minutes late. We got on famously. He had a slouch like me, red eyes, a flannel shirt, crappy jeans, greasy hair, baseball cap and no ambition whatsoever. Of course, he couldn't start work until he had smoked a bowl so we stepped out back, tucked behind the propane tanks and caught up on things since high school. There was nothing new to speak of except that he was growing his own weed. It was very low grade shit so he smoked it constantly. He had joints in his wallet, a one hitter in his pocket, a pipe in the glove box, a plastic bong behind the couch at home.

The night crew consisted of me, Pothead, Rice Cooker, Night Watchman. Rice Cooker had the only important job in the plant and he knew it. He kept himself smocked up and knife edged regarding the cooking of the rice – he ran five minutes ahead of the watch on his wrist. Night Watchman was his complete opposite. He sat in a lunar eclipse in his Monte Carlo on the plastic tarps out back – the first and last order of defense against the anarchy of time. He followed his 2:00 a.m. snack with a long nap – something I took notice of right away. "Hey, Pothead, check out Night Watchman snoozing in his car again. He's got the best job in the plant."

"No shit?"

"Yeah, he's got the car running, the heat on, snoring to his favorite tunes."

Every so often the wild rice arrived at the plant in gunny sacks so they were dumped directly onto the plastic tarps. At night Pothead and I would cut them open and shake out the rice and rake it over. We were doing just that when 2:00 a.m. rolled past. "Hey, Pothead, how much are they paying for this fucking rice at the gun shop?"

"I don't know, about a buck sixty a pound, why?"

"Wanna make a little money?"

"How?"

"Let's drag a couple of these sacks into the woods. We can come back this weekend and snatch them from the other side and sell them at the gun shop."

The edge of the woods was about thirty strides from where we were working. Pothead was thinking, screwing his face up trying to crunch the numbers, swinging between greed and apathy. I gave him a nudge, "I'll bet these bags weigh sixty to seventy pounds each. Dude! We're standing in a pile of hundred dollar sacks."

"What about Night Watchman?"

"It's almost two-thirty, he's asleep, believe me, but just in case let's take a closer look."

We ran up and got a shot through the windshield, so close we stopped breathing. We waved our hands to see if he noticed. He was fast asleep in the Monte Carlo, idling its life away in park. What you do to yourself you do to everything around you. His lunar eclipse was a black hole, it depressed me and pulled me toward the center. His god-awful snore vibrated through the glass while the valves of his heart and the engine's lifters clickety clacked in the background – they were running low on oil.

Our breath returned in shallow steps as we ran back to the gunny sacks, grabbed one each, pulled them about twenty yards into the woods and stuck them behind a dead tree. We popped out of the woods in a full adrenaline rush – hyper alert, eyes in the back of our heads – drowning a quick breath to listen for a sign of anything. There was nothing out there. The Monte Carlo and Night Watchman were still dying and so were we, but it was less obvious.

"Two more!" yelled Pothead. Why the hell not, we're just now beginning to breathe, great gulping mouthfuls of air went straight to our heads. We each grabbed another and stacked them like sand bags behind the dead tree. Back on the tarp, I went over the rest of the plan with Pothead, "What is it, Wednesday? Let's meet up on Saturday night and drag them out of there." Pothead wasn't listening, he was caught up in the moment, bouncing up and down, as dark as the trees, greasy hair flapping and flopping on his flannelled shoulders, lifting his helmet and raking his scalp with resin laced fingernails. Suddenly he was ambitious, "Two more, man! I wanna buy a hookah!"

"Listen dude, let's not get too greedy here, maybe if another load comes in we can grab a few more. A little at a time is best." I learned that from the Old Man, expect things to go bad any minute; the demon groans – shifts its weight. In a flash, the Old Man could be on top choking the life out of you – it was right there always right there. You learned to tiptoe – if you wanna live – you learn to tiptoe.

Pothead yelled, "Fuck yeah!" as he lit a cigarette, hands shaking, excited, too excited. I got a funny feeling. I wished I could take it all back. "Hey Pothead, remember, you can't breathe a word of this to anyone." "Yeah, yeah, I know." Twenty minutes later, in the break room, he almost spilled it to Rice Cooker. I had to choke him off and misdirect the conversation to keep him from giving it away. Pothead: "Hey, Mick, I think I will buy a hookah after we sell that fucking rice." Rice Cooker: "What the fuck rice are you talking about Pothead?" Pothead: "The rice we're gonna sell at the gun shop." Me: "That's right, we're gonna get out on the lake tomorrow and harvest our own wild rice." Rice Cooker: "So you're spending money you don't even have yet, huh, Pothead? Harvesting wild rice is hard work. I don't think you're up to it." Pothead sat with a giveaway grin. Lucky for us, barrel oven number eleven was calling, according to the clock in Rice Cooker's head. I decided right then and there that it was either think of something quick or decline to see it through.

The next evening as soon as Pothead arrived for work, I peeled him off to the side and acting all agitated told him that the boss had found the gunny sacks in the woods. "Night Watchman insists that it didn't happen on the nightshift, swears he was wide awake all night. It looks like they believe him." Pothead was relieved, "Goddamn, that was a close one wasn't it?"

"Yeah, no shit, I'm just glad it's over I don't think I've got the stomach for it anyway."

"Yeah, me neither. Hey man, you wanna get high?"

"No doubt about it."

With Pothead out of the way I brought my old pal Country in on the situation. He was mild mannered, a bit of a risk taker and he wouldn't blab it all over town.

Come Saturday night, we slogged along with our flashlights in the stinky woods through an unnaturally warm autumn mist – a pail of piss. We carved a crescent moon through the underbrush looking for our dead tree in the land of dead trees. They're not really dead just mortally wounded – they gorge themselves during the short ninety day growing season – the bark cracks under the pressure – sap bleeds down the trunk – a twenty mile an hour gust snaps them at the stem and the pulp bursts into the sunlight.

We found the gunny sacks and soon discovered that they were soaked through from the pissy rain and relentlessly heavy. It was a good half mile of crescent moon between the rice and my trunk. My lifelong anti-work ethic meant trouble for me from the start. I was weak. I couldn't carry both sacks at once so moved them one at a time down the same broken path. I quit every couple steps, sat on the sack and moped and groaned, "Fuck this shit man, I'm done." Country was faring much better than I. He laughed and pushed and prodded, "Hey, Mick, this was your idea, stop whining about it and get moving. I don't want to be out here all night." We crawled down the crescent and up the other side and, at the last minute, one of my gunny sacks ripped open on the end point and most of the rice poured out onto the ground, but I didn't care anymore.

Sheba

Winter. Country and I still had a little wild rice money left so we packed like lower class tourists and bummed a ride to Minneapolis from his dad. Between us we had enough cash for two plane tickets and one month's rent somewhere. We picked Orlando because it was south and the next flight out. We landed at two in the afternoon and were drowning in the mugginess by two-fifteen. I wanted out of there, "Let's try the Southwest." There wasn't any money for that so we finagled a subcompact rental and went on a three day car tour of lesser Orlando – palm trees, concrete, swampy green, nothing else.

We slept in the subcompact on our backs, with the seats reclined, in the fucking heat. Only alcohol helped, but not much. We picked up a newspaper and found a month-to-month rental that would take us. It was a big old house that had been split into four no bedroom apartments. We got a ground level quarter-section. We slept heads to toes on a Murphy bed that fell out of the wall and laid there twisted and lumpy – we did the same. The bathroom had a naked bulb with a string hanging from the ceiling. You had to sweep the air in the dark to find it and when you pulled and released, the giant cockroaches would scatter. My instinct was to attack anything smaller than me. I went after them with the bottom of my shoe and smeared several along the wall.

The other ground level quarter-section was occupied by the caretaker. He was an ornery drunk. He kept a German shepherd staked in the yard right under our window and it barked and growled nonstop. Every now and then Ornery Drunk would fall out of his backdoor and argue with it like a spouse. "Sheba! Goddamn it, knock it off you fucking whore!" Sheba howled. "Sheba, you know I love you, but if I let you inside you'll shit on the floor and they'll kick us out of here. Sheba don't you understand?" Sheba yelped and growled. "Oh, Sheba sweet Sheba, my love Sheba. I'm going back inside now darling. I'll see you in the morning. Goodnight sweetie."

Ornery Drunk harassed us day and night. He caught us coming and going by keeping a whiskey ear to his yellow door. If he saw so much as a newspaper on the floor he'd give a fifteen minute drunken lecture as to the fire hazard we were causing, then threaten bodily harm and eviction in a halo of whiskers.

I got a job as a busboy at a place called Valentine's in downtown Orlando. It was an upscale bar/restaurant that featured live soft pop jazz for the suit and tie crowd and their girlfriends/secretaries in slinky dresses. They sucked up booze, steaks, seafood, cocaine, and stabbed each other in the back on the way to and from the toilet. They laughed hysterically at everything under the sun except themselves. Regarding their own comfort they were dead serious. If every little thing didn't go their way they'd abuse the staff and storm out without paying, proving once again that the more money you have the less you're likely to pay.

Every Monday night from seven to nine it was free champagne for the ladies. They trampled in from the street in their slinky dresses and dumped it down their throats and soaked themselves with champagne piss and champagne sweat and champagne puke. They screamed for our gay champagne waiter

"Aldo!" "Aldo!" "Aldo!" "Over here! Aldo." "Pour us some more champagne, Aldo." Gay Champagne Waiter pushed through the wall-to-wall dresses with two bottles lifted over his head and, while the ladies held their glasses aloft, he filled four at a time out of each bottle with a twist of the wrist. Back in the kitchen he wouldn't conceal his contempt, "God! Those girls are disgusting pigs."

The men in suits arrived on the scene and circled like sharks, sipping whiskey, eyeballing the slinky dresses, slicing through, sniffing out the most drunk/least judgmental. By the end of the night, all the ladies were tanked and it became a feeding frenzy. The sharks took what they wanted. One shark in particular was simply outrageous. He'd hover outside the women's bathroom, stop every slinky dress on the way out, make a play right then and there and if she was drunk enough he'd drag her to the men's room and fuck her in a stall. The pissing sharks would circle in front of the stall, sharing snickers and teeth and winks, secretly hoping she'd pass out so they would all have go at her. She'd exit at some point biting her lip, straightening her hair. She wouldn't look happy or the least bit satisfied about what went on in there, but such is the life of a champagne lady in a slinky dress.

I got out around 3:00 a.m. – after the last pile of champagne puke was mopped up and the wait staff had given the busboys a little slice of their tip money according to their whim. The walk back to my little quarter-section took me past an urban cowboy bar where it was free beer night for the ladies. I stood in the shadows and watched the drunken cowpokes in the parking lot go at each other with lips, fists and dicks.

Back at the quarter-section Country was on his fifth sleepless night, by day he was a dishwasher. He wobbled in the kitchen sprinkling rat poison on raw hamburger meat, "This will stop that goddamn dog for a little while anyway." He was also decorating the walls with a magic marker and dumping everything on the floor. I adjourned to the pull-string-bathroom and chased the cockroaches, then added up my tip money. It wasn't much.

Sheba ate up all the hamburger and by morning she was lying on her side bloated and wheezy. Ornery Drunk went into a grief rage, doubled his usual intake, howled, barked and scratched at our door. We didn't let him in, the place was beyond anything he could take.

One day we were out walking along and found ourselves in the black quarter-section of town. It was late in the afternoon and everyone was hanging out on the sidewalks and there was music and barbecue blowing out of every shack and big black men danced together in front of barbershops and said from the deep gutter, "Whaz up fellas?" as we passed. I said to Country, "They have practically nothing and look how they're enjoying life – what gives?" He didn't know. Suddenly, a '64 Chevy, rusted blue 4-door, cruised up just behind our left earlobes, four young men from the neighborhood, about our age. There was no exchange between us – they couldn't find our eyes and we couldn't find theirs. We fought to keep our leisurely pace – they pushed us forward. They discussed things amongst themselves. We couldn't make it out. They revved the '64 Chevy, jerked it up even and laughed and mocked our profiles. We politely acknowledged the truth; they had us if they wanted us, but they didn't want us.

We wandered back to our quarter-section and trashed the place some more. By the end, we were wading through newspaper confetti and every wall was full of our angst and dark humor. We scrammed out of there upon notice of eviction. Ornery Drunk hammered it to our door with a sixty-penny spike – his happiest day in recent memory. We pulled the door closed behind us and gummed up the lock, just for the hell of it, then headed for the Greyhound station.

Hitchhiking Story No. 0

The first time I stood by the side of the road and stuck my thumb out I didn't believe I would ever get a ride. I asked the ditch weeds, "Someone is gonna stop for ME?" It was beyond possibility. Then it happened and I was thrilled. All the way to the passenger side door I was the happiest man in the world, then, I got a look through the window and my euphoria collided with the thing behind the wheel. I kept a finger on the door handle for the first twenty miles.

I can tell my whole life's story in ten miles or less. I'm good at sizing people up – the gleam in the eye – the bend of the head – steering grip – twitching hips – hard on the gas – quick to the brake – lead in the ass – fools on the take – button down shakes – quivering quakes – poison intakes – rods out of place. Me: freezing – drunk – sliding – praying – peeling – sighing – sneezing – coughing – riding – always riding.

There is magic in motion. It comes from the friction. Gravity is life – you have to fight it – keep moving – the illusion takes care of itself – it rubs off on everybody – you have to live – it can be a tidal wave or just a drip drop drip drop – an entire life – drip drop drip drop – most live in between – like a penny under a cushion, barely worth picking up.

Gray angels are calling me in from the frost bitten world, but I can only see them when I'm fully loaded and then they're so beautiful and they breathe into me and I rise up with them and then I think, a few more drinks and it'll be even better. They dump me off on the corner of black and blacker – something something in the morning – I never wear a watch – never ever ever ever wear a watch – you'll only end up killing each other. Too late to realize that zero is the only number that really matters.

Hitchhiking Story No. 1

Country and I ended our Greyhound tour of Florida in Daytona Beach. A few days later we had patches of sunburn where we refused to pat each other down. Broke, we were bounced out of our little beachfront balcony by hotel management. If you have no money, you're not welcome anywhere. We hung on for an extra day by squatting on the beach, dining and dashing the Pizza Hut. The dream of seeing something was gone, so with suitcases and duffel bags in hand, we headed for the road out of town, made a bet as to who would get home first, then split up on the freeway onramp. Country moved further down the line – he slouched along the gravel strip with his battered luggage, his straw blonde hair waving in the wind.

It was early Sunday morning. The hung-over good Christians were on the way to church, they were in no mood to help out the needy. A few of them still had enough in them to give me the finger as they passed – it was one last little thing…

When I was a kid, the church we attended was tiny, white and Lutheran. The Mom picked it out of habit – a gift from her long suffering mother. We shared our Pastor with another tiny church out towards Aitkin. He had to cover both, we got the early shift – 8:00 a.m. sharp – with Mrs. Germaulous on organ. At the door they handed out a stapled down program filled with promises and commands and complementary hymns. We filed in separately and worshiped the same way. We had the usual off-key assortment and one really good singer, a blonde woman, younger than the Mom. She sang above everyone – no one got in her way – she was nearly perfect. She had the cutest damn family of the well adjusted: proud Father Type at her side, a gaggle of button nosed kids and a crowd of admirers after every service. One day she found it all lacking and left her pitch perfect life and shacked up with a Hung-over Lover who lived just three doors down. They met out by the garbage cans. It was a scandal. They kept on coming to church though, droopy Father Type and a gang of troubled kids on one side, Blonde Singer and Hung-over Lover on the other. She still sang with all her might, some things were never gonna change, everything else was different. At the end of service there was no longer a crowd. It was just her and Hung-over Lover standing around, flabbergasted by the lack of response, like her voice wasn't attached to all that other crap.

Sunday school was held in the basement. We sat on folding chairs at an equally foldable bumpity table. Each table came complete with a dolled up member of the assembly. We colored in Jesus with waxy crayons. I was a piss poor student, I blended Jesus into the background with the darkest hues. Dolled Up Member saw a pattern, tried to take me under her wing. She had nice wings.

I rose to the top of my class. It didn't take much. It was the Mom's only wish that I would stick it out 'til my confirmation. Then I'd be saved no matter what. We filled the front pew – small town fourteen year olds – hicks in clip-on ties, yellowed shirts and oversized dress shoes. The Pastor waved us to our feet and prearranged positions, then smiled benignly and tested us in front of the congregation regarding various historical facts that Lutherans deemed worthy. I was the only one who'd studied (always been a sucker) and it was apparent to nearly everyone, but they dutifully ignored it. I was the only one giving answers, at first competitively, then after question number six, more and more reluctantly. I held my hand down until the last possible moment, my classmates were dazed, heads bent, eyes glued to the floor. They couldn't remember anything, let alone the Lord's Prayer. It was up to me to make us look good. The Pastor was the last to notice my solo gig (he was a dreamer) but when he did, he cut me off in mid answer, cleared his throat and suggested a hymn that was already in the program. Mrs. Germaulous fired up the organ and we were waved back to our seats where we were to remain 'til the end.

We were the first to leave. We went forward past the podium to a door in the corner that led down to the outside or further down to the basement. We chose outside and gathered together in the gray gray gray and consoled one another with stinging backslaps, cuss words, feats of tucking and rolling. An elder statesman suggested a road trip to a bigger town. There was only room for him plus four more and there were twelve of us trying not to look interested in case we didn't make the cut. Elder Statesman chose his drinking buddy first, then me, then Stevie and Jimbo (two of my cronies). We rode in the back of a rusted out mid-sixties Charger. No girls were invited – we were gonna talk about girls – we couldn't have them about. It was the go-go Seventies – the girls formed their own posse and followed us around, drive-by harassing. We ignored them at first because there were some bigger town girls stroking the sidewalk with bellbottoms. We cruised by slowly trying to look cool with our yellowed shirts and squinted eyes, but our local girls kept revving and honking their beetle bug at us. We responded with cutting insults and bare asses and middle fingers and Johnny Rotten sneers until they drove away sulking. The bellbottom girls, upon seeing our ridiculous behavior, turned their backs on us as well. I was the most disappointed of all because one of them had just made my list and I didn't know her name. A beautiful girl without a name, I invented a naming game to pass the wintery nights. I put them on her like hats – tried to match the sound with the face, there was no telling. I was systematic, started with 'A' and worked my way through. I went around twice then ended on Veronica. Oh, Veronica, I'm so tired of the one channel, the six foot drifts, the gray gray gray, the Old Man on parade, the Mom stirring the gravy.

When we were sent to summer bible camp, classes were held in the same tiny church basement. We Elmer-glued Popsicle sticks into manifestations of Jesus and the gang, cotton balls became beards and hair. There were little plastic bowls that sat in a row down the center of each foldable table; they held gold and silver sparkles for all the glorious things. Every couple hours we were released to the vacant lot next door where we beat on each other in the name of Jesus Christ our Lord.

At noon they brought out sack lunches and we picnicked in the dirt: peanut butter or bologna, an apple, a tiny bag of chips, a stale cookie and a can of purple Shasta 'cause that's all they had so be thankful for that. The Prime Director would talk us through the ordeal with half-assed observations that wound up comparing everybody to Jesus. He put us one on one and we didn't match up very well, "Hey, Mick, I saw you pick your nose and eat it. Do you think Jesus would pick and eat his own snot?"

"No, Prime Director."

"Rusty, I saw you take an extra cookie. Do you think Jesus would take an extra cookie?"

"No, Prime Director."

"Sally, I see you peed your pretty dress. Do you think Jesus would pee on himself?"

"No, Prime Director."

"Of course not, this should be a lesson to you all. You'll never be perfect like Jesus but you sure can try. Now let's get back inside, today you'll be making your very own Ten Commandments calendar."

"But there's twelve months in a year, Prime Director."

"We'll make it work, don't you worry about that."

He shuffled us back inside. It was another hazy summer day lost forever. My calendar ended on Thou Shalt Not Steal...

I tried to seem pleasant from the side of the road, but nobody was interested. I stood on the gravel strip for over two hours – played tic-tac-toe in the dirt – my right foot versus my left. Finally, a rusted-on-through Camaro pulled over. I ran up and popped the door part way open and asked, "How far are you going?" "North Carolina," said an iffy son of a bitch. I was tired of standing there and willing to take almost anything – this was it. "Mind if I throw these in the backseat?" "No fucking problem."

I flipped off Country as we passed him by, half hoping he'd remember the car I was riding in just in case I was never seen again. He was standing in his spot on the gravel strip with a sour face and sore thumb. Iffy asked, "Is he a friend of yours?"

"Yep."

"Well, I ain't giving him a ride."

Iffy made it clear, he was fresh out of prison and heading back to North Carolina to kill his former best friend and anybody who got in the way. I knew he was serious, or at least, for the moment. His head was a perpetual motion machine, not smooth and flowing, but all herky jerky, like he was trying to catch me out of the corner of his eye in the act of something that he could take personally.

"And do you know how I'm gonna kill him?" He mimicked a gun with his fingers – the thumb was the hammer, he flicked his wrist to fire it, "Bam Bam Bam right in the motherfucker's head! To do what he done to me and s'pect me to take it like a pussy!"

There was no talking sense to a guy in his frame of mind. I decided to cheer him on, keep him thinking about that, no time to think of me and my unworthy life. To stay alive until the next intersection was my goal. I got right in front of Iffy in order to avoid the corners of his eyes. I stayed dead center, "What'd the son of a bitch do to ya?"

"That son of a bitch stole my woman while I was in prison and knocked her up."

"No shit? That son of a bitch has it coming then, doesn't he?"

"Hell, yeah, he does and you don't wanna know what I'm gonna do to that bitch when I get a hold of her."

I jumped in and over-did-it, "You should gut shoot him, then slice him up with a dull knife. You know, make him suffer before you finish him off. That'll teach that son of a bitch to fuck with you!" I gritted my teeth and made stabbing motions with my hand. Iffy gave me a good long look – dead center. I sat tense in the cracked bucket seat. He said, "Yer all right," and went on with his story.

Twenty minutes later a car pulled up next to us in the passing lane. It was Country riding along in a lime green Gremlin with a good looking blonde girl. He lifted a bottle of beer and took a big swig, while the girl cut a big smile across my lap, hit the gas and disappeared over the horizon. Iffy summed it up, "Looks like your friend got the better ride."

Understatement of the year.

Hitchhiking Story No. 3

I stood next to the freeway on a late Sunday morning in Jacksonville. Church was out for the week and I was ducking all the shit the good Christians were throwing at me from their cars as they passed: shoes, beer cans, clothes hangers, insults (near as I could tell anyway), bibles, cigarettes, cigarette lighters, Rand McNally's, crayons, trees, buildings, lakes, mountains, manifest destiny. History itself came tumbling out the windows of America's sedan-wagon-pickups, all of them riding the horn.

A fat bald middle-aged man swung to the side in a brown Dodge Dart Swinger. He was a regular southern belle with a little mint julep smile, furtive sidelong glances, all shy and retiring. I was up to my neck with these oddball characters lately – cosmic cows – always wanting something while pretending otherwise. I was in no mood to play with this ray of sunshine. He didn't know that. "Mmmm, it's almost afternoon. I'm getting hungry. Are you getting hungry?"

"Yeh, sure"

"What say we find an exit and have a bite to eat, my treat."

"Yeh, sure"

"Say, there's a Kentucky Fried Chicken, does that turn you on?"

"Yeh, sure"

"Okay then. I'm so happy. It's Sunday, hallelujah, and I've got a new friend."

We went inside. Sunshine was warm and hazy and unable to decipher the Kentucky Fried coded menu. "How does this work? I've never been to a place like this before." Me thinking, of course you haven't, sweetheart, you were probably born here.

Back on the road, Sunshine tried to pull me out of my shallow grave. "You're probably broke aren't you, dear? Hitchhiking is so dangerous you really should fly back to, where is it? Min-a-soda? I could help. I have a business and I'm looking for a sort of Guy Friday, you know, like a Girl Friday. I feel like taking a chance on you, you seem so nice. You could help me run errands, that sort of thing. I'll put you up in a hotel and in a few weeks I'm sure you'll have the money to fly back to, where is it? Was-con-son?" He was excited, probably thought it was in the bag. He spilled, "You know, I'm very happily married and I have two adorable kids, but sometimes, I like to give blow jobs. Would you like a blow job? All you would have to do is lay there."

"No thanks."

Sunshine clouded over and pulled off the road. "You'll have to get out here. I've got places to go and people to see."

I didn't like that idea. I didn't know what road I was on. I reached out and grabbed him by the side of the neck and said, "Listen here, Sunshine, I'm going to get out my map and find the road I need to be on and you're gonna drive me there or I'm gonna take your car and drive there myself – got it?" Sunshine wheezed out an affirmative. I let him go, grabbed my map and pointed the way forward.

We hit the I-10 westbound and I told Sunshine to pull off and, through some impulse, I demanded his wallet. He handed it over without a word. I grabbed the cash, stuffed it in my jacket, took out his driver's license and threw the wallet in the backseat. "I'm gonna jot down your address just in case you try pulling any shit." Poor Sunshine looked so damn pouty. I thought about his wife and kids, if they were real, they didn't deserve this. I gave him back his money and that cheered him up some. He shook his sad, fat face and said something about never again.

I didn't believe him.

Michael McDaeth

Hitchhiking Story No. 5

I walked the northbound ramp to I-75 with a thumb out and was picked up by a college kid in a jacked-up Nova headed back to school in Valdosta. A weirdo, shrill, silly, temperamental, chatty, and a bragger on top of it all, but what could I do? I was the passenger – the ride along – just a minute before, I was on the side of the road with nothing but my clean cut.

Weirdo claimed his old man was worth millions and he could have whatever he wanted whenever he wanted it. Everybody has to have something. Then he said he would refuse all of it and suffer for all mankind – he was an opera of jagged lines.

I detested the very people who were willing to give me a ride. I was living off, even depending on, the bottom feeders, in a country full of riffraff, who were willing to annihilate every living thing while yawning something about the inevitability of it all.

Weirdo got it started, "Where ya headed?"

"Minnesota."

"Wow, you have a long way to go. We flew into Minnesota once, on my father's private jet, but I was there to feed starving babies."

"Oh, yeah."

"Yes, my humanitarian work sure keeps me busy. Oh my god, I am so craving fresh lobster."

He kept slanting his eyes my way just like Sunshine a few hundred miles back. "So, what do you do in Minnesota?"

"As little as possible."

"I hear that. With my money I'll never have to get a job – ha ha ha. That's why I'm in school. I am not interested in a career. I want to help the less fortunate – that's why I picked you up."

"Oh yeah."

"Yeah… So, do you have a girlfriend?"

"No, but I'm looking."

"Yeah, me too. I broke up with my girlfriend a couple months ago so I'm really on the war path. I was just down in Jacksonville for the game, Gators vs. Bulldogs. Oh, if that ain't a football rivalry! There were hot chicks everywhere and I nailed a few, of course. Anyway, there's a big blow-out party tonight at my friend's sorority, would you like to come?"

"A blow-out party on a Sunday?"

"Oh yes, we do like to party at Valdosta State. And the girls in this sorority are hot hot hot. You can crash at my place if you want."

I was hoping to cover more distance but it was getting dark and the idea of having a roof over my head for the night was appealing, even having to deal with this millionaire nut. "That sounds good to me."

Weirdo lived in a shitty little bungalow (not much for a millionaire's son). I took a shower while he cooked a frozen pizza. We met up in the kitchen and ate the pizza and drank a beer. I was anxious to get going, "What time does the party start?"

"Oh I don't know, I suppose we could leave soon."

Weirdo seemed bored with the topic but I persisted. "How about now? We can pick up some more beer on the way."

"Oh all right then." He struggled to his feet clearly perturbed, me thinking, I'll push this turd out the door if I have to. I made him slam a couple beers and that helped immensely – he was beginning to blink. "Where's your fucking car keys, Weirdo? Let's hit the road." I let out a "Whaa-hOOOoooo!" as we headed down the street toward sorority row.

We pulled up, no party in sight. We climbed onto the porch and thumped on the door. Five minutes passed. I was prepared to stand there all night. Finally, three sorority sisters opened the door in their nightgowns. Weirdo took the lead, "Hey there, Melody, I thought you girls were having a party this evening."

"We were, but we all got so drunk last night we're just completely out of tune today so we decided on a lazy day instead." She glanced at me and asked, "Who's yer friend?" I jumped in, "I'm from out of town and I'm staying the night here in Valdosta just to attend your party." All three girls gave me that oh you're so sweet look then sang in unison, "Oh you're so sweet." Melody said to me, "Would you like to come in off the porch?"

"Yes, would any of you like a beer?"

"No, thank you." The party ended with a crash.

While Weirdo was playing rich-man/holy-man in the front room, I felt an urge to turn towards the staircase that ran down from the second floor and spilled into the next room. Standing at the bottom of the staircase was my dream girl in a flimsy nightgown – it was see-through so I couldn't help myself. We locked eyes. We were twin souls from the tin void, echoing off the hard pan for a million lifetimes in the dark, the cold, the loneliness, the futility of it all. But now we saw each other for the first time, in the light, the heat, the love, the wonder of it all. Suddenly, Weirdo grabbed his gut and said that he had to go – couldn't wait another second – out the door he went. The three sorority sisters snapped me out of time and pulled me toward the door. Again in unison, "You better hurry, Weirdo's real sick." They pushed me over the door lip and onto the porch before I could hit the brakes. As I spun around I saw my love, as the door was closing, smile and sing out, "Maybe I'll see you tomorrow." I sang back, "Yeah, yeah, yeah, you'll see me tomorrow and every day after that." I bounded off the porch with a whole new life running through my head.

Back in the car Weirdo was still clutching his gut, but the closer we got to the bungalow, the less he complained. And just as quick, was his old annoying self, "So, you made quite the impression."

"Who was that girl by the staircase?"

"I'm not sure. I think she's a freshman, why?"

"No reason. Hey, Weirdo, do you mind if I hang around for a couple days? I think I might like it here, you're a good guy, and everyone seems friendly. Maybe I'll check out the school."

"Stay as long as you like – it's not like I can't afford it – my place is your place."

We arrived back at Weirdo's and by then it was getting late. I was busy planning the rest of my life with Dream Girl when Weirdo, unable to penetrate the fog, decided to hit the hay. I fake yawned and crashed on the couch – still spinning with Dream Girl. Thirty minutes passed, I had her wrapped in a satin sheet on the couch next to me, then came Weirdo from his bedroom calling my name in a way that didn't sound right, "Mick..." Dream Girl slid off the couch and into the dark. Weirdo again, this time from the doorway of his room "Mick... Are you awake?"

"What's up, Weirdo?"

"I'll suck you off if you wrap me in cellophane." Then he threw in, "How about I give you a thousand dollars for some fun – you'll like it I promise."

That pissed me off, "You can't buy me!" I went hard-ass on him like I did with Sunshine, "Listen ya son of a bitch I'm not into that kind of shit and I'm sick and tired of all you fuckers hitting on me."

Weirdo blew a fuse, "What do you mean fuckers – fucker! I don't need this shit – get out! – get out of my house!" He threatened to call the cops – the militia – whatever – if I didn't get the fuck out.

There was nothing left to do so I asked him for a lift, "Hey man, it's a hell of a walk, at least give me a ride to the fucking freeway." Ten minutes later I was on the side of the road contemplating the Georgia dirt.

It turned into a cold, wet, goddamn night and there was almost no hope of getting a lift. Only three cars passed in three hours and anyway, no one was gonna pick up a stranger in the middle of the night. I hunkered down in the ditch, smashed apart, my beer buzz gone, done in, never to see Dream Girl again.

Daytime took its position and I went back to my post and took it like a man, a man on the side of the road, broke.

An old fella in a Buick slid over to the side. I sprinted for the door with suitcase and duffel bag flapping at my sides, moving again. Old Fella was only going to the next exit, would that be good enough for me? The point was to move move move – ten feet, three thousand miles, whatever. I hopped in. "Where ya headed son?"

"Minnesota."

"Jesus, son, you got a long road ahead of ya."

"Yup."

Less than a mile later "Well, this is where I get off, sorry I couldn't push you a little farther down the road."

"Yeah, me too."

"Well, so long and take it easy."

Every ride was like that. All morning long, one exit at a time through southern Georgia.

A tricked out little Datsun pickup with a topper pulled off and the guy on the passenger side jumped out and directed me to the rear, "Hop in the back with the other guy."

Sure enough, there was another road duck leaning on a backpack. He had a flask of sipping whiskey in his hand. I climbed over the tailgate. Passenger side guy closed the topper, bounded back to his seat and we spit a little gravel at the ditch.

The road duck offered me a drink, "Here, take a swig." He was road hard with tar under his fingernails, windshield glass in his heart and a pair of sunken headlights staring at me from under a greasy hat. He was alright. He was more than alright, he was free – free from all encumbered crap – free to sip his whiskey while others drove – free to speak his mind – free to hold the truth. He seemed the average bum. He didn't have a home, just a few drop off points. He called them wide spots in the road. He came back from Vietnam and kept on going. He held no resentments, grudges, disagreements, debts, loves, interests, money, pain, or heartache. He shared his whiskey generously, but mostly sat back smiling at the passing day.

It was late afternoon when I climbed back over the tailgate and stood again by the side of the freeway, the north side of Atlanta entering rush hour. It was much worse than the Sunday I spent trying to get a ride in Jacksonville. People swerved their cars at me, threw half full bottles of beer, etc. Murder hung in the air, a tangible thing. They plowed through it and it clung to their faces and arms, squirming their skin like maggots. They screamed on by with a, "Get a horse, motherfucker!" Then, the rush hour peaked and the traffic came to a standstill and they just sat in their cars discussing me in murderous tones, deadly stare downs, sinister guffaws. A car full of look-a-like jocks had a conversation amongst themselves as to whether or not they should cut me up and leave me in the ditch. No doubts that anyone would come forward and report the crime – they were all in it together. I wobbled on the side with a headache and stone lips. I had nothing to say to any of them. If they wanted to come murder me, they were welcome to try. I imagined taking each one of them down with me – numerous dirty tricks to even the odds – anything goes as they say. It began to rain – it was an acid rain.

Hitchhiking Story No. 7

My rain dance attracted an old geezer in a '54 Ford pickup truck. We checked each other out and agreed that it would be all right. "Young man, I do believe this is your lucky day. I have never in my life picked up a hitchhiker, but you looked so goddamn pathetic I figured this was as good a day as any to break with tradition. In fact I ain't entirely sure I didn't just dream you up, what do you think about that?" Old Geezer twinkled like a morning star – his eyes shot right through me. "I'm as real as they come," I replied. He said, "I'll be the judge of that," and stomped hard on the brake. My skull went into the dash – snapped back. "Yep, you're real all right."

Geezer was cruising back to his farm and it was a good stretch of road so I got a chance to settle back, rub my forehead and enjoy the ride. As we climbed out of the greenest valley in the world, Geezer unfolded the story of his life in light waves. Each one rolled over the top of me, overwhelmed me. I could only catch little snippets. His dead wife wore a sunflower dress and a pile of curls. She was his recipe for life. He met her at a square dance – buckled her down tight while she kept him on the straight path and that taught them both a thing or two. They stood by the river year after year and it was grand. "There is nothing greater than love, young man, remember that."

Geezer dropped me at his exit and there I was again. I took position, stuck out my thumb and stared at the sun through closed lids. It was just bright enough to almost feel warm – a place to dream, but I didn't have any dreams, all I had was a beginning.

I was pulled out of the Mom – early evening, early summer, early sixties. The Mom was a smoker, her milk was radioactive, above ground testing was still the fashion. I couldn't drink her milk, so they put me on powder and water and by the time I was three years old my eardrums had exploded from the toxic buildup and my fetal position. Luckily, it was the perfect condition for those cold northern Minnesota winter nights. Nothing escapes the clawing ice crystals, all sound is sucked out of the air – even the air is sucked out of the air. Over the years, I choked on chimney smoke in the winter and weed pollen in the summer, but it kept me alive.

Standing at the edge of the woods – woods I could see right through to a field of starving corn and our neighbor, Mister Mower, firing off rounds in twenty-two caliber, the long ones. He wasn't the only one. Everyone was shooting at something. At times we mistook each other for dandelion, raccoon, muskrat, bunny rabbit, and fired away in every direction. To be clipped off at the ear suited me just fine, to feel a bullet whiz past, to reside at some distance from the screaming of the Old Man.

I could see the demon in the Old Man's eyes. It had him and he had It. It gave him stomach ulcers. It kept him from murdering me – so there was an upside – he wasn't in the mood – he couldn't bend over. The Mayo clinic removed the ulcers. The demon stayed on, smoldering, just under the skin. I had the idea It would leave the Old Man any time either one chooses – neither one ever chooses – but they could and that was the point…

A late model sedan churned the loose gravel next to me and a hard ass looking old man at the wheel gave me the once over and demanded, "Hey! You in the army?" I looked at him with a painted stupid grin, "Huh?"

"The fucking bag stupid!" He pointed his index at my army issue duffel bag.

"Oh, no, I bought it at a surplus store."

"How far are you going?"

"Minnesota, sir." I threw in the "sir" thinking, That'll get me off this fucking gravel strip.

"Minnesota!? You're a good goddamn long way from Minnesota." He was a one star General looking for an argument. He was the kind of man who pulled you into a conflict, then blew his top and accused you of starting it. "Get in I'll take ya up the road a piece." I hesitated. "Don't argue with me, goddamn it, I ain't got all day." He plucked the lock and I climbed in and we tore out of there leaving a future watering hole in the loose gravel.

One-Star General was driving to the prison in Vandalia, Illinois to see his one and only son. I thought to myself, So, One-Star General sired a convict, that's what you get when you bring home boot camp to the wife and kids. Served him right anyway, all the able-bodied boys he broke down, probably jacked off to the thought of it. He continued the assault "What the hell ya doin' in this neck of the woods anyway, are you lost?" It's best to agree with a high-ranking arguer, it drives them crazy when you don't give them a fight.

"No, sir. Unless you say so, sir."

"Who's your God?"

"Your God, sir."

"The apple doesn't fall far from the tree."

"You're right as rain, sir."

"Where you coming from?"

"I left Daytona Beach a few of days ago, sir."

"You are not making very good time."

"You're right, sir."

"Of course I am right why wouldn't I be right?"

"Yes, sir."

"The last time I was wrong you were in diapers."

"Yes, sir."

It was a monotonous ride and it wasn't long before One-Star General was looking to dump me back on the side of the road. "Goddamn it, that kid of mine isn't going anywhere. Think I'll head south to Abilene and see my yellow rose." It sounded like a load of bullshit. I almost suggested that I had an uncle, I was dying to see, who lived right there in Abilene and that I would love to ride the whole way with him. That would wind him up a little. The thought of this fake little shit-stain singing poisoned honey "Yes sirs" in his ear the entire trip down would make that one star shine out. I'd drive him down a fox hole with my sweet smile – push him over the top – charge! – anyone who disobeys will be shot on sight – Freedom ain't FREE! Motherfuckers! Nah, better to get out before the flash-back and anyway I didn't have any choice. One-Star General pulled off, I got out and stood on the gravel strip with my duffel bag and suitcase and watched him drive away right back onto the northbound lane headed for the penitentiary. It's pain to lose such a long ride even when it's a shitty one – almost anything is better than standing on the side of the road.

Hitchhiking Story No. 9

I squatted on the gravel strip until 3:00 a.m. The wheel was on the downside – what little traffic that rolled past acted like they didn't see me – so lowdown in my life. I started walking toward the bright lights of a truck stop a couple exits over. Low low low. I trolled the truck stop parking lot for a good Samaritan, "Hey mister where ya headed?"

"Milwaukee."

"No shit! I'm heading in that direction myself, can I bum a ride?"

"Nope, sorry, the company won't let me. Liability issues."

The same old story from every one of them – company men to the core, "What happened to Rubber Ducky?" I implore. "Never was such a thing," they retort, "jump a train, you fucking wart."

No train in sight, I shuffled back to the freeway and walked and walked and walked all the way to a rest area where I spread out my army issue sleeping bag on a concrete picnic table and dropped out of sight. A couple hours later I was back standing on the freeway – thumb up in the cool dawn air – barely refreshed. Hardly a dip from the well and still I was on my feet, dancing in the morning sun, happy, so very goddamn happy – for no reason at all.

It took forty-seven rides to go a couple hundred miles. The day was gone, the moon was rising fast. I stood and sat and stood again. Nothing, just me and the moon waiting for a tardy hunk of Skylab to tumble out of the sky, not a doubt in the world that it would hit me. Only the moon would see it, a mute witness to my last moment, cracked square in the skull, split down the middle.

It was at least two in the morning when one of those mid-sixties GM model spaceships went wheezing past, muffler dragging on the pavement, a comet tail. The suspension was shot, so the body was riding the axles like that murderous hunk of Skylab in a coffin. It squeaked, wheezed and sparked as it ground its way down the ramp and onto the freeway. Then it stopped, reversed, and wagged and dragged its way back up the ramp. I dove for the ditch. They found me anyway, cracked the window, "Which way is Earth?"

"You're already there."

"Do you need a lift?"

"No doubt about it."

The dust cleared as I made my way to the passenger side door. There, with the window cracked wide, was a shit-eating-grin wearing a very drunk spaceman. I queried, "How far are you boys going?" I got a glimpse of the captain at the controls, he was just as dizzy as Mr. Shit-Eating-Grin. He pointed at the moon, "We're going that way – hop in."

I climbed in the back and sat, tense, in the middle between my duffel bag and sunflower suitcase. Captain had a hell of a time counting us down. To his credit though, when he hit zero, he found the gas and we jerked out of there and nearly went off the ramp before he yanked us back on course and we wagged and dragged our comet tail down the ramp and into outer space. Captain needed the entire universe to keep us moving forward and, if that wasn't bad enough, both of them wanted to talk with me so had their heads twisted toward the backseat, mouths flapping. I couldn't make out a thing they were saying, something about light years, black holes and hand grenades. I leaned forward between them and tried to tune them in. Captain was on fighter pilot, Skylab was strafing the Milky Way. He kept screaming at me in that over-enthused-falling-apart-alcohol-fever-way you get before the hammer falls. He slapped the steering wheel around like it was a heavy weight prize, a prayer wheel, a mail-order bride. Shit-Eating-Grin was trying to light a cigarette with his head out the window. Planets zoomed by in the background, zoomed by again, and again – like a cheap cartoon. There was a halo over Skylab though we hardly deserved it, drunken spacemen-angels of Babylon and I.

The effect of Captain's twisted head caused Skylab to veer excessively to the right. Since I was the only one looking forward, I was the only one who was terrified. I pointed past his starry eyes, "Look out!" He jammed the wheel to the left just in time and kept it out of the asteroid ditch – without even turning his head! Oh, sweet halo, hang on! Shit-Eating-Grin yelled, "This is our planet!" and Captain brought it out of warp and dry docked it at the top of the ramp. I bailed out just as the Tennessee Valley Authority pulled up behind with lights flashing and siren blaring and out came two hard-assed aliens with their guns drawn, kicking up quite a stink regarding our re-entry. They slipped me and my baggage to the side, after ten minutes of sober pleading, and hauled Captain and Not-So-Shit-Eating-Grin off for a night of quarantine and six months of counseling. I was left with a warning to, "Stay the fuck off the freeway, punk." Which I returned with a, "yes sir," followed by a slightly delayed, just above whisper, "motherfucker."

After the cops cleared out, I popped the hood and stood next to Skylab hoping for a sympathy ride. Someone from the first car that passed hollered, "Get a horse." I laughed and yelled back, "Yeah, that's original!"

I had a horse once when I was a kid. I was shoveling horseshit in the corral one day when the Old Man said to me, "The next one's yours." It was his attempt to heighten my interest in his mini ranch. It didn't work, but some things are just meant to be. When the foal was born she turned out to be just as sickly as I. She wandered around the pasture coughing and wheezing and dripping. We were a perfect match, cross species soul mates. We walked around the pasture together, wiping our noses on the same tamarack posts. I hardly ever threw crabapples at her and when I did, I went easy on her. The Old Man couldn't take it, the horse reminded him of me and I reminded him of the horse. One of us had to go, it was a toss up. Then, the side of her neck started to swell. It looked like she tried to swallow a watermelon. The Old Man called in a veterinarian, but he didn't know what it was. He suggested we contact the veterinary school at the University of Minnesota since they were always interested in rare cases.

We hauled my sick little filly down to the school and on the way there the Old Man got me all worked up, "I don't know why we're doing this, I doubt she'll live another day." Suddenly, that horse meant everything to me. I sobbed out the window. The Old Man gave me a couple minutes, that was all he could take, "Oh, quit your blubbering, it'll be alright or it won't."

The veterinary school determined that my horse had an infected guttural pouch caused by a little rip in the throat that allowed a little dribble of her mother's milk to collect and spoil and swell. They closed the gap and drained the pus and soon she was just another healthy, happy horse. I was alone again…

The next car to appear slowed up and rolled down the window, "You having some car trouble?"

"Yes, I am, can you give me a lift?"

"Sure, how far ya goin?"

"Minnesota."

"Jesus Christ, boy, I'm only going ten miles."

"That's good enough for me."

"Well, climb on in then."

Everybody talks about how wonderful this country is but I gotta say I don't see it. I'll agree its natural beauty is quite stunning, but wherever we've setup shop, put down roots, blah blah blah, it's disgusting. Talk about the banality of evil, the same scene repeats itself every three miles: a rolling crooked frame – coming or going it's the same bowel movement – the same fucking sale – used car dealership – fast food – motel – gas pump – pigpen – supermarket – split level – alcoholic. Progress is an eye sore.

Hitchhiking Story No. 11

The road was barren, again, nothing but a chill wind blowing down my backside. I was on a long trek down another northbound freeway and in one of those, "How in the hell did I end up here?" Moments of despair. My life was full of them. I swore if I ever got back home, I'd never hitchhike again. It's a goddamn losing proposition.

While I was shuffling, shivering, dragging, sniffing and sneezing, a sixteen wheeler pulled off to the side of the freeway, stopped, and swooshed the airbrakes. I took off running for it. It was farther than it looked. I ran and ran and suddenly found joy in my legs, pumping up and down, kicking the gravel strip. I was chasing a woolly mammoth over an ice planet, I was racing the unwinding clock. I felt footsteps behind me – they were real, unforgiving, un-repentant, fast, aggressive, deadly, thundering the gravel strip. It sucked the joy out of me. This was it! Everything depended on me winning this fucking race. I kicked my legs high, strained my neck, gritted my teeth, but the footsteps were still gaining on me. I felt a hand or a claw or a dagger or fangs, reaching. A last shot of adrenaline pushed me forward – it gave me super strength and rubber band legs. I slang shot the distance to the truck with my chest puffed out in one great last breath and crossed the taillight as the driver was coming around the end. He jumped, man, did he jump, and when he landed he yelled, "What the hell was that!?" I was busy gathering my senses, "What? You saw something?"

"Oh never mind, what the fuck are you doing out here in the middle of nowhere anyway?"

"I'm heading up North, can I get a lift?"

He gave me the usual once over, looking for something out of place, some sign of crazy that would tell him to move on without me. I kept mine well hidden most of the time.

"Well, fuckin' A, then, I suppose I can give you a lift – you don't wanna be out here. Something's not right. I'm heading to Chicago. I've got some early morning deliveries to make, if you help with that, we're even."

Chicago! After toiling away for days, weeks, months, years, I was finally getting somewhere. I'd help deliver anything to that fucking city: illegal aliens, a trailer full of cocaine, riot police, votes for the Daley machine.

My new trucker buddy was the largest pear shaped man I've ever seen. He was all bottom, yet he stood over six-four. He was also extremely agile and incomprehensibly light on his feet. He practically floated above the ground.

In his big rig, he was constantly on his CB radio, "Break one-nine, this is Arkansas Zig Zag, I'm riding high in my semi – just passed mile marker 55 northbound on I-57 and need to make up a little time here. What's the Smokey situation out there? Come back." I found my Rubber Ducky! No one answered his call. He got pissed quick, "Goddamn it! Are ya'll dead out there or something? Give me some goddamn help, here." Through the speaker squawked, "Aaaah, hey there, buddy, I seen a bull in a plain brown wrapper around mile marker 78 heading south, not five minutes ago." Zig Zag replied, "Thanks good buddy. Say, what's your handle?"

"Just call me Pete." Zig Zag looked over at me with disgust, "Alright, Pete, have a good one, I'm out." He clipped it back in place, pulled from his pocket, a little tin box with a sliding tin lid, took out a tiny white pill, popped it in his mouth, and sucked on it like it was a candy mint. He called them head pills, he didn't offer me any, but he did pull out a joint, "Hey where you headed anyway?"

"Minnesota."

"Minnesota, eh? Now there's a state I can't legally drive in."

"Oh yeah, why not?"

"I was in court there in the Twin Cities contesting a fuckin' speeding ticket some stupid fuckin' cop gave me. Anyway, my license was revoked for contempt of court."

"How fast were you going?"

"How Fast!? I was turning a fuckin' corner in downtown Minneapolis and that stupid fuckin' cop pulled me over and said I was doing over forty miles an hour. Well, I went to court and told to the judge, there ain't no way in hell that you can turn a fuckin' corner in fuckin' downtown Minneapolis, at forty fuckin' miles an hour, in my fuckin' rig, without fuckin' rolling it on its fuckin' side.

"It's simply a fuckin' matter of fuckin' physics, there's just no fuckin' way to take a fuckin' forty-five degree fuckin' turn, at over forty fuckin' miles an hour, without tipping the fuck over. I told the judge, my fuckin' rig's outside, let's fuckin' jump in and I'll fuckin' show you! But he kept on fuckin' hammering away, fuckin' telling me to fuckin' tone down my fuckin' language. Tone down my fuckin' language!? It fuckin' don't matter if I'm fuckin' cursing. I'm fuckin' right, goddamn it! Listen to the fuckin' facts."

He could really get up a head of steam, he waved his arms around, popped another tiny white pill, and yelled about not being able to drive legally in half the fuckin' states.

Zig Zag had stories, lots of them, I could hardly contain any of them, I was so road beat. I slipped in and out, his stories were inspired hallucinations – I was a little man hiding in his shirt pocket – he strummed his guitar fighting for peace – the judge was a crow – the jury was meat.

Zig Zag was back on his CB radio, "Break one-nine this is Arkansas Zig Zag riding high in my semi, anybody out there? Come back." A woman's raw smoked-out voice crackled through the speaker, "Hey there, Arkansas Zig Zag, this here's Baby Cakes, down here at Bill's Truck Stop. What can I do ya for?"

"Baby Cakes, I'm having some trouble. Ya see, my trailer brakes keep locking up on me and I need to get em' fixed ASAP."

"Where ya headed, honey?"

"I'm northbound on I-57 just past mile marker 120."

"Well, darlin', you're in luck. We're just south of Effingham. Roll her on in and we'll get our mechanic on it right away."

"That sounds like a date, Baby Cakes, I'll see ya in thirty, over and out."

"Honey, it's not a date until I get a good look at 'cha."

We pulled into Bill's Truck Stop around two in the morning, dropped the trailer, and went inside for something to bite – burgers and fries – burgers and fries – gravy gravy gravy – coffee coffee coffee coffee coffee. Dead eyed cowboys and bona fides turning phrases – plaid faces – teeth missing – growling and hissing. The bare naked lights beamed into my mind, a two million watt light bulb burning in my head. I was about to fall off my stool when Zig suggested I catch some shut eye in the sleeper because he was gonna spend time with Baby Cakes. I bailed out, cracked my face on Bill's fucking glass door, staggered to the rig, climbed up inside and fell out of it.

The bed was comfortable. I felt for a rusty spring poking through the middle. Force of habit that started when I was a kid and almost every night the steady drip of my sad, pale, piss soaked through the fabric and spiraled down rusty springs. Eventually one of the springs broke away and poked through the mattress, right in the middle of where I slept. I tried to tape it over, tuck it back inside. Its altitude and disposition employed a portion of my waking mind at all times. But I was a deep sleeper, a heavy dreamer. I'd toss and turn and the rusty spring would record it on my back, front and sides. A bloody trail of tears – an algorithmic statement of fact. Other nights it would unwind itself and jam an end into my spine – a spinal tap tap tap. Lord knows if the other end of the rusty spring wasn't strawing in the piss puddle under the bed...

Zig Zag popped the door open and brought me back to the tin void. "The trailer is ready to go. We gotta make time if we're gonna beat the morning rush into Chicago and we don't want to get stuck in that fuckin' mess."

Zig Zag's massive country music on cassette tape collection beat a steady path to the playback slot machine – it was a convoy – heartache doled out on razor thin tape. He held them up to the light to get a better look, "I think this is Marty Robbins or is it Charlie Pride? You know, that nigger can sing."

We rode the rest of the way with little conversation between us. A rain began to fall. The road was dark and wet. It was that time of the night when even if you're awake you're quiet – the world just goes on without you. You dig deep down into your thoughts, nothing out there except the rain, the thump and squeak the wipers make, the diesel moaning about something, the Doppler effect of each passing wreck with its requisite pair of hands, eyes, ears and feet, the parting of a black sea through the gut of Illinois – so full of Midwest cheap, so full of grief.

Morning broke up the night and scattered the rain. We'd slipped into Chicago before light and were waiting at the loading dock of a warehouse deep in the underbelly, used to be part of the stockyards or so I was told. It still had the stink. Zig Zag's head was piked to the end of a worn-out spring. It kept his face from falling in his lap, but that was about it. 8:00 a.m. clicked into place and the warehouse door opened only as wide as was necessary. Zig Zag put a kink in the spring, popped another head pill, grabbed his clipboard full of invoices and receipts, and jumped down out of the rig. I followed suit. We climbed the stairs to the usual dry, hung-over, working-class greeting and commenced with the distribution of things. "Check the label, is it ITF Corp?"

"No."

"Then push the fucker aside. What's that one say?"

"ITF Corp."

"Don't just stand there, put it on the dock. Let's see here, seven boxes on the invoice, seven boxes on the dock. Sign here, and have yerself a good one."

Down one side street after another we hauled our load, goods and services on the prowl, invoiced, tagged, tampered with, deducted and certified for the consumers. So they can put on their britches, climb out of their bomb shelters and stumble on down to the stockyards where they'll be sliced open with a dull knife and stuffed full of rubber chickens.

With the last delivery delivered, Zig Zag was ready to fly high in his semi back to Arkansas. He pulled through some toll booths, zig zagged to the edge, reached out and we shook hands. I got my first look at him in the broad daylight. He looked like a wipe out, a ten car pileup at the end of a black sheet of ice – deep sad eyes and road rash up, down, and across his face. It was a beautiful song – it was a song about death.

Hitchhiking Story No. 13

I thumbed a sweet ride with a typical traveling salesman who was on the road pretty much nonstop, rarely picked up hitchhikers, once in a while took a chance, never had a problem. In fact, he liked the company and since I didn't look so bad he took a chance on me. We chatted about the weather, this and that, and pretty much melted into the pavement as we passed the day traveling through the Wisconsin countryside.

At the end of our time together, Traveling Salesman pulled out his wallet, handed me sixty bucks and said, "It is too damn cold to sleep outside so get yourself a room and some dinner and good luck to you and have a nice life." I wasn't used to people being so generous for nothing – I tried to resist, "Ah, man, you don't have to do that." His reply, "Every day, someone, somewhere, saves your life, most of the time you just don't know it. Now, take it and get out of here."

It was a few short strides to a motel. I got a room, then wandered over to a Country Kitchen on the other side of the overpass for my burger and fries.

Back in the motel room I paced back and forth. The loneliest room in the world is a motel room. A room should have a sense of permanence to it, a place where you can put it in Park, a sanctuary away from everything until checkout time. There's no getting comfortable in an American motel room – it's built to push you along, the thin pillows, towels, blankets, walls, and toilet paper tell you the truth, "Give us your money and go to hell!" The only way to get any sleep in a motel like that was to get drunk and I did. I sang to the waning moon through the thin curtain.

It was my first musical performance since I was a misfit fourteen-year-old at a family reunion, folks from the Mom's side of the family, unbearably happy, drinking, undeciding, fundamental, inward bearing, mostly. Around the campfire, in a field behind the barn – an RV Park for the long weekend. Uncle Something stumbled up, "Let's have some music!" The Old Man squinted at me through the fire – I could tell what was on his mind – that devilish gleam meant something, always.

The Old Man did not drink but once a year, he chose this night. He thought about my incessant playing on a Buck Owens red white and blue, all-American acoustic guitar – all the aggravation it gave him watching his "Bonanza". He wore tight fitting cowboy boots and demanded that his children be the boot jack, "Hey, Mick! Get yer ass over here and pull my boots off." He made me straddle his leg with my back turned and, while I pulled from the heel, he pushed off on my ass with his free leg. When the boot was about half way he gave me a good shove and sent me on a header across the room. Then he laughed, pretend apologized, mocked delighted, rubbed it in my face.

Now he was demanding that I play, for the campfire crowd of relative strangers, a song of my own selection. We knew what this meant. I didn't know any covers. I was fourteen, I had a one track mind. I'd taken a couple lessons from a music store musician. He attempted to teach me rock 'n' roll riffs by Zeppelin, Black Sabbath and Aerosmith. I'd spit them back differently and he would get all upset, insisting I buy a metronome, practice the scales. I quit taking lessons from the music store musician. I was working on my own tune by then, "Broken Roses" was the title and it was awful, but I thought it was one of the greats. The lyrics went something like, "Broken roses, broken roses, I'm not upset about broken roses – broken roses, broken roses, I don't give a shit ("crap" – if I knew someone was listening) about broken roses." On and on it went like that while I pounded out various contortions on my smashed up, out-of-tune guitar.

So the Old Man called me out with grunts and groans while the relative strangers colluded with whoops and hollers and ridiculous clamor. I was trapped – the Old Man was ecstatic – the Mom looked worried – the sisters were glad it wasn't them. When I got up to go to the house everyone cheered and then the Old Man sang out, "Bring me back a beer from the fridge." I took my sweet ass time, went over my lyric sheet, tried to tune my tuneless guitar, grabbed a can of beer and dropped it on purpose, twice. I returned to the fire with my laminated plywood guitar and a medium gage plastic pick. I handed the Old Man his beer and he set it on the ground next to his lime green plastic lawn chair. My place by the fire was taken by skinny pimple cousin and it seemed everyone had forgotten about my performing for them anyway, so I retreated to the outer ring and stood just out of the light.

Within minutes a dull moment arrived and the Old Man yelled for me front and center and said, "Don't just stand there, play the goddamn thing." Everyone agreed. I closed my eyes and laid into "Broken Roses" with all my might and mangled my way through a verse and a half before I snapped the G string. I stopped in mid swinging sentence, my eyes shot open, I glanced about at everyone still frozen in the flames – the Old Man was about to release. I wound up, swung again and started screaming, "Broken Strings Broken Strings, I don't care about broken strings." Then I ended it in a five string flourish and everyone laughed and applauded. Except the Old Man, who would have none of that good ending.

"Put that goddamn thing away before somebody gets hurt. If I knew you were playing like that I'd have stopped buying you strings a long time ago." Everyone laughed at that as well – they were an equal opportunity audience. The Old Man was just warming up. He reached down for his beer and plucked it off the ground without even looking. He was looking at me, demon eyes shining, ready aim fire. He held the beer on his knee and popped the tab. Beer shot all over him – everyone laughed – it was so goddamn beautiful – I can't even begin.

Hitchhiking Story No. 15

A crazy loon in a rust bucket plucked me off the side of the road. He was bee lining it to the Twin Cities, late for work, all worked up, hated everything. His rust bucket had holes in the floor, you could see the passing street. When it rained, the bucket would fill from the bottom up. There was always a puddle, a pond, a lake, depending on the thaw in the early spring. He stocked it with fingerlings – they ate at your feet – he fished them out in the fall and grilled them like steaks.

Crazy Loon was frustrated. He no longer migrated. He commuted between two meager points. He was to get everything he needed from that. He knew it wasn't a passing phase. He even knew there was no getting out of the way. Still, he wasn't going to be late. Not too late anyway, he was doing 88 in the left lane, on a frozen road of cracked ice. Crazy Loon's rust bucket transferred its weight up through my brittle bones and shook off the shattered glass from last night's gutter walk. Back to its usual size the world still looked the same – flat.

We passed some rusty trailer homes, sitting just off the road, with driveway, mailbox and power pole. I lived in a trailer home for a time. It was situated along a stretch of road that ran parallel with some railroad tracks, east to west and vice versa. The front of the trailer had a big bay window that faced the road and railroad tracks. I was three years old. My thrill was feeling the rumble of an approaching train through my feet, shimmering my legs and vertebrae then out the top of my head. I'd run to the bay window and watch the train pass. Sometimes it was a passenger train with people looking out. We'd wave to each other and smile and laugh and make faces and they'd take a piece of me and I'd keep a piece of them and tingle all over and find that I had pissed myself again. The Mom was kind about it. She'd boil up some water, pour a hot chocolate, drop in a giant marshmallow and set it in front of me. I'd sit there, stuffed up and dripping, and push the marshmallow under with my spoon and watch the hot chocolate rise to the rim and spill over the side. I'd catch it with my tongue. The side of the cup burned. I'd complain but keep on flicking my tongue. The Mom would intervene, "That's enough now, dear. Go outside until it cools off."

I'd step out the door and sit on the fold-away step and prop myself with elbows and knees and hands and cheeks and imagine being on a passing train, sitting next to the wavers, smiling at the blue sky while passing by all the other rusty trailers just like mine: sagging – carved out of the wonder – so matter of fact – the concrete slab – the patch of burnt grass – the rusty barbecue – the assorted broken clutter – the mud gravel driveway – the constant puddling – the handmade sailboats – the green army men with submachine guns, pistols, bazookas, jeeps, tanks, lined up against the plastic Indians frozen in mid tomahawk chop or bowed arrow. I'd move to my self-propelled scooter and make my rounds – up one lip of the driveway and down the other – lord of the clatter – the undertaker – the ultimate decider – waiting for the next train…

Crazy Loon refused to come to a complete stop, no time to spare. I had to jump out when it looked safe. It never did. I grabbed my shit and threw open the door when the son of a bitch took a hard left and kicked me out into the street ass-over-head-wards. I landed on my back and rubbed a rash to the side of the curb, still holding my crap. I bounced up in a crowd of do-gooders and pretended I was okay. I smiled obscenely through the pain and stiffed it onto the sidewalk and muttered obscenities for relief – it hardly helped, but it kept me moving north. I could almost smell the Mom's bacon grease. I hopped a city bus with some loose change. Only 160 miles to go... minus 3 blocks and a stop... minus 6 blocks and another stop. A man in a wheelchair got on. I secretly grieved for him even though he slowed me down. I gave him my sincerest smile, my eyes of encouragement, my nod of hope. He thought I was ridiculous. Only 160 miles to go... minus 9 blocks and another stop... now the wheelchair was getting off! Maybe I'll get off as well and push him off a CLIFF!

Hitchhiking the road had me really jacked up. I animal tracked the other bus riders through their stink. I sat behind a girl with long red hair. I didn't get a good look at her but I knew she was in heat – her musk was drifting under the seat – I got a boner just sitting in her stew. I felt like talking the bus driver out of the wheel and driving it myself. I'd drop everyone off, of course, even the bus driver. But I wouldn't let anyone else on. I'd ask Redhead to stay on 'til the end. I was sure she would agree – tis' the season.

Michael McDaeth

The Septic Tank

I hunkered down at the mini-ranch in the long flurrying winter. The snow doesn't pile up like it used to, but it's still bitter cold at the bottom of the bulge that distends from the Arctic Circle. I slept the days away on the rusty spring and dreamt of nothing that I can remember.

At night, Country picked me up in his gray truck and we rode along with dim headlights, drinking high octane alcohol and concocting crazy kicks on the fly. "Hey! Let's get some bows and arrows and shoot at sixteen wheelers from the side of the road. Think about it – they'll get to where they're going, get out, and see some fucking arrows sticking out! It'll be great."

"I know the perfect spot."

"Let's do it! Whaaa-hooooo!"

With bows and arrows in hand we hid in the tall weeds and thin snow where the sixteen wheelers slowed for a curve in the road, just outside of town. Every few minutes came the lonesome whining retreads, the leaning gearbox, the staccato throat of the vertical pipes "pfffffpapapapapapapa." We bent in ambush, pulling back our bows, shaking in anticipation and then, there it was passing like a great beast of the road. 'Whoosh' we let our arrows fly and saw them stick or thought we did – it was a black moonless night. We were up and down, laughing, yelling, screaming, doing mock imitations of our victim's supposed reaction upon seeing the arrows sticking out somewhere down the road, "Wha tha!? Well, I'll be. I was attacked by Indians."

We shot twenty arrows into ten trucks and, on the last one, we were so drunk and hyped up we sent our arrows into the driver's door and he locked up his brakes and nearly jackknifed on the corner. We tore out of there, a two man drunken war party, back to Country's gray truck. "Did you see that!? Did you see that!? Did you see that!?" It was too much. We hit the bar and our friends gathered around for shots and beer chugs and one of them asked, "What've you guys been up to?" "Oh, just a little big game hunting."

The Old Man frowned at me through my hang-overs then took some time away from the horse collection and his job with Inter City Natural Gas and went to a horseshoeing school in Oklahoma. He was still trying to create his beloved 1870's. He dragged the Mom along for safekeeping. I was left in charge of the mini-ranch. I was feeling especially good about myself for some reason. I got drunk as hell every night. I threw outrageous parties in the barn. I brought in a couple wood-fired cast-iron stoves and set them too close to the kindling wall. People came from all over to tear off a little piece of the mini-ranch to take home, smash on the ground, bury in the snow. The cast-iron stoves overheated and set the barn on fire. It filled with smoke, but nobody fled the scene. They threw beer on the flames and held their ground – there could be a lawsuit. Eventually, I came along and put them out with a few shovels full of snow.

Sometime in early June the Old Man returned with his graduation certificate and the Mom still in tow. He didn't like that his barn had caught fire or that there were tire tracks all over the big lawn. It happened one mad spring night during one of my all-night beer brawls. Two hundred violent offenders showed up that night. I built a huge bonfire under the yard light and had four kegs on ice. Some bad acid was passed around. The beer was going fast. The driveway was full of fistfights. Someone tried to take off with a tap and keg. We caught him and he got his.

The party went on and on while the Bad Acid Drinkers stared into the bonfire or leaned against invisible walls. The beer was long gone, except for the trickle in their cups, yet they refused to go away, so I filled a ten gallon bucket with ice cold water and threw it on the bonfire. A tidal wave of wet ash rose up and did smite the Bad Acid Drinkers. That bummed their high even more and it didn't help that I was laughing. The bonfire was out cold. One of the Bad Acid Drinkers threw their trickle of beer in my face, under the flickering yard light, and screamed, "You ruined my fucking jeans and my fucking life!" The rest of them screamed and hollered, then, stormed to their cars parked on the big lawn. The frost was fresh out of the ground, the Bad Acid Drinkers sunk to their hubcaps trying to get back onto the driveway. They splattered mud and ripped gutters into the lawn before catching the gravel and making their getaways through the pioneer gate. A couple days later, I filled in the gutters, raked them smooth and threw down some grass seed. The grass came up a much darker shade of green then the rest, so you could see where the gutters crisscrossed the lawn like some mad slashing razorblade to the arm. The Old Man didn't see the humor in it, "Why didn't you have the parties in the house? Hey! Someone drove over the septic tank!"

"Yeah, that was a rough one. It was completely out of my control."

"If the septic tank is ruined someone's gonna have to pay."

"Tell you what, I'll hang around and help out this summer."

"Goddamn right you will."

I spent the summer dragging my ass around the mini-ranch. I put in a decent effort, but the Old Man was quick to disagree and make something of it. He was in an active period, where every little thing had to be done right, his way, busy, busy, busy. He wore me out just looking at him.

One mid-summer day, I was lying on my back, on a bending slope, bending the tall grass, a bad angle for the sun most of the day – it stayed damp, yawning, dreamy, cool in the mugginess. My slanted eyes watched the building clouds building to something, dark and heavy, just out of reach. The sweet breeze that kept me in place disappeared, replaced by nothing but a vague muggy threat.

The Old Man stepped out of the house and saw the open corral gate. His horse had run away. He blamed me as usual. This time he was right. I did it on purpose. "Go! Run free in the parking lot." I heard the neighbors screaming over by the railroad tracks. Ah, there she is – My Babe's Bear, a registered Quarter horse, a buckskin mare, a born rebel.

The clouds continued to pile up – up, up, up. The sudden stillness suddenly terrified me. I got to my feet and wandered into a patch of trees. I followed a well worn trail toward the back of the barn. I was almost there when it broke open, a rush of wind out of the west, bending the tree patch. I ran for the edge, bent for the house.

The Old Man cut me off at the step, "You left the goddamn gate open and the horse is out again. If anything happens to her you're in for it." The phone rang through the mosquito screen. The Mom came to the door. Neighbors on the phone – horse last seen heading down the railroad tracks, eastbound, running with the wind. It began to howl, the downpour was coming, a smell like life and death together in the same drop, musty, hot, clammy, cold.

I worked my way toward the basement through the dust, but the Old Man caught me, "Get in the truck we'll cut her off." He split a perfect curve in the gravel with his three-on-the-tree heading for the Deerwood shortcut around elbow bends. I locked the door and contemplated the seat belts. They were buried under extra coats, battered hats, scrapers, clipboards, salt starched gloves, lighters, crowbars, quarts of oil, brake fluid, pistols, coffee mugs, an owner's manual, jumper cables, a gas can, gas man equipment and my ass. We never wore seat belts – ever.

The horse could only move east or west along the railroad tracks. The sides were mostly oil slick swamp filled to the rim with greasy frogs, greasy ducks and Red-winged Blackbirds bending the cattails, but not in that breeze. We picked her off at the nearest crossing. She contemplated the swamps for a getaway then attacked us with her teeth. The Old Man sidestepped and got her by the mane, slipped a rope around her neck. Her time was up. I walked her back down the tracks. The wind was gone. The rain was torrential.

The Turkey Plant

I landed a job at a turkey plant about one hundred miles south of the mini-ranch – still cold as hell. A former classmate invited me down for a look around. He had an extra cot along with two other roommates in a basement. The landlady lived upstairs. "It'd be nice if we could split the rent four ways instead of three." It was to his credit and self-interest that I got the job. He advised me to give them a call the day after my interview. "They like it when you check in with them – makes them think you've got ambition."

He was right, the secretary said it herself when I phoned, "The manager said the first three to call in were hired. You're number three. Show up tomorrow at 6:00 a.m. sharp."

The turkey plant was stuffed with blue collar girls, more in common than not, hardly a fresh face in the rafter. They leaned on their elbows in the break room, puffing cigarettes and drinking coffee, asses as broad as the chairs. They'd have left a long time ago except they were supporting families of one to seven, including a husband or live-in boyfriend who used to work at the same turkey plant, but had long since been fired for incompetence or insubordination; men have pride, women have work.

I was attached to the other two call-ins, Bent and Brat. We looked each other over, did our best to stare each other down. We were ordered into the plant to find the turkey ham manager. The administrative assistant plotted our course, "Go through that door, all the way down the hall, all the way, don't worry about the other doors just keep going all the way, then left, take a left – show me your left, okay – after the left there's another long hallway, this time half way down, the third door on the right, take it, you're almost there, go two thirds the way down that hall, take another right, you're in your last hallway. At the end you'll see double doors, that's where you'll be working, he should be there as well."

We took a shortcut because Brat (he called in first) wanted to, "If we go through here we'll cut off half the building." We got turned around, then there was a dead end hall. We stood at the end of it and traded guesses, "Which way next?" There wasn't much choice, there was only one other door. We entered and stood before a line of hefty bags sucking the guts out of thousands of turkeys with industrial vacuum cleaners.

The turkeys were hung by their feet on hooks that traveled along an overhead track. Their living to dead, to plucked, to sliced up or ground down, was only three minutes forty-seven seconds – this year's goal was three and a half. As the turkeys rode along the track the hefty bags went at them: stabbing cavities, raking skin, pulling, sucking, preening – the filth, the smell, the splatter. We walked along the outside wall – single file like Vietnam. We lined up like we called in and passed through like pale ghosts to the other side of the wall and there was the turkey ham manager. He'd come looking for us and, now that we were together, he led the way. Brat was second in command and somehow Bent had fallen behind me – it seems I was bumped up the totem pole. The truth is, you don't even have to try in this world, just fill a spot, appear agreeable and throw out an answer every once in awhile. It doesn't even have to be the right answer, they'll glom onto anything.

The turkey ham manager was a Golden Retriever. He was excited about life, it was in his step. Down the long narrow company corridor he wagged his tail, bounded ahead with ears flopping, bounded back with tongue hanging. He was a happy dappy Golden Retriever. "Come on guys just a little bit further. This'll be so great – you guys are gonna love this job! Now, it might take a little bit getting used to." He jogged backwards, shuffled sideways, hopped up and down. I leaned into Bent, "What other tricks does this little fella know?" Bent straightened up and let out a chuckle. Golden Retriever changed directions in mid hop, ran back, jumped up and placed his front paws on Bent's shoulders bending him back in place, "I love your enthusiasm this morning, Bent, keep it up." Then he jumped down, scampered around a corner, popped his head back and said, "This way guys, we're almost there."

It clicked in my head. That's the line they always use: from every atom, to condom, to rubber suit, to metal box, to prison cell, to clock radio, to every charge of a light brigade, to every missile dropped, to phone calls, to houseboats, to freeways, to airplanes, to cancer, to heart disease, to starving kids, to murdered wives, to smokestacks, to guns, to knives, to brides, to chiefs, to vice, to pain, to mass murder, to broken feet, "This way guys we're almost there." In this case he was right. When we turned the corner, there was the machine ready for meat.

There are worse things than living in a basement. We labeled our food, counted our slices, drew lines on the side of our milk cartons. I watered down the liquor. We smoked upper-Midwest ditch weed and traded in dizzying conversations of our self-interested selves from which we seldom strayed. Where we overlapped we practiced social upheaval, more or less filled the space between us.

Cuddles and Catholic, the other two culprits in this basement, helped balance the teeter-totter and we went at the booze and weed and coke with an all out effort – it was here that we wished to be employed full-time but, as they say up North, "You can wish in one hand and crap in the other and see which one gets filled first." Alternate ending: "You can clap all day."

Cuddles was the tiniest bodybuilder in the world and he had the tiniest dreams besides. He spoke of his muscle car in flexed tones as he flexed for his reflection, he was barely bigger than a breadbasket, "Candy apple red with a lacquer finish, that's what she's gonna get soon as I rebuild the motor and put on the new headers." He was the first to fall asleep on his cot. Less than forty-five seconds after his head hit the pillow his little snore would drift over the other cots. Knowing how easy it was for him to sleep made it impossible for the rest of us to sleep. We'd lay there astonished, impressed, puzzled. "How does he do it? Has he no worries at all to rack his brain for at least an hour every night?" "Maybe he's a goddamn saint." "No, more likely a thoughtless idiot." We'd laugh and then Catholic would complain about his fiancée and we'd laugh some more.

Catholic was tall, blonde and permanently engaged to his high school sweetheart. She lived miles and miles away in their hometown. One would guess she was ruffled in feathers, eating bon bons, putting on the first of many layers, sitting on the parent's couch, watching her stories. They worked on the wedding plans and their troubled relationship at the same time over the phone. You couldn't tell whether they were breaking up or picking out the flowers, it was the same argument. He'd slam down the phone, "Goddamn it! she drives me crazy." Every other weekend he headed home and they argued in person.

I followed my hangover to the turkey plant and bombed through the morning – endless turkey hams linked in fours and pressed in twins between rectangles of spot welds and steel. We sprung them down at the corners and slid them onto a rolling rack. In the dull, forty-degree, turkey plant conditions, my head floated off my shoulders and rose above the florescent lighting.

From there I could see a hot summer day I spent as a five year old kid when we lived in town on Main street. The Old Man forced me outdoors to the back alley and dirt parking lot. He told me to use my imagination and make it fun, "Keep your eyes peeled for any rabbits." I did more than that. I dug potholes and threw in carrots, lettuce and celery, and covered them with sticks. I sat on the steps and waited. The noise of summer played in the distant background, only the voice in my head was clear and it didn't know what it was talking about. Some alley rats came passing through, spotted my traps, gathered around and asked the obvious question. I gave the obvious answer, "I'm trying to catch a rabbit." Oh, what a laugh they had. The biggest alley rat set me straight, "There ain't any rabbits around here." They laughed some more and kicked the dirt in my direction and asked if I was born in a barn. I didn't know. I tried to seem thoughtful. I gave it serious consideration then said, "It's certainly possible." That sent them into orbit – they did an Indian dance around my traps. I got up, climbed the steps and went into the house. The Old Man was lying on the couch. He cracked an eye, "Hey, Mick, who are your little friends out there?"

"They aren't my friends."

"The hell ya say." He had that gleam in his eye – he was a demon cat, "No one said life was gonna be easy. Stop being such a goddamn baby!"

I went to the window and stared out, the rats were just leaving. The Old Man got to his feet. He didn't like that, "Don't be such a chicken shit, get your ass back out there. It's a beautiful goddamn day and you're missing it. If anyone gives you any lip it's best to go down swinging." He opened the front door and pushed. I landed on the bottom step.

I spotted a daddy longlegs making his way toward my bottom step. I stalked him, followed his path with my eyes, pulled him out of a dirty little dark corner and dragged him to the nearest rabbit pit. I brushed away the sticks and scooped out the carrots, lettuce, and celery and dropped him on the bottom. He ran for the wall, but he didn't have a goddamn chance. I grabbed a leg, snapped it off and watched it wiggle in the dirt, unattached. I dove into the pit and cleared a side of him and watched him spin in a circle like a runaway clock. I went back to the step and found another, and another, and another, and brought them all back to the pit and ripped them apart in a hundred different ways, but it was never enough. "It serves you right!" I could hardly breathe.

I filled in my pits, but you could still see the scars where the bottom reached the top. I swore off animal cruelty, took my revenge more directly by propping nails against the tires of the Old Man's truck. I snickered and cried and went into the house. The Old Man was just leaving. I thought about running back outside and removing the nails, but it was too late, he was moving fast.

I raided Big Sister's room for some reason. I didn't know why, just felt like doing it. Her Easy-Bake oven was great, I smashed it. The Barbie kitchen and bedroom was pretty cool, I fell on it. She had a row of stuffed dolls on her bed. I picked up the Raggedy Ann and looked her over. I tucked her under my shirt and went back to my little broken down room. Everything in my room was ripped apart, experimented-on or smashed to pieces. Raggedy Ann was the best thing in the place, so neat and tidy. I cleared the crap off my bed and set her on the pillow and jabbered away while I straightened up the place. I pushed all the broken pieces under the bed for the piss-fed alligators. It was a new start – just her and I.

Next thing I knew, Big Sister was screaming in the doorway. She was out of her mind. She charged and knocked me to the tile and scratched and punched and screamed 'til the Mom pulled her off. I pretended I was really hurt. I rolled out the big tears, the big show, until the Mom said we were even. Big Sister took back her Raggedy Ann. As she was leaving, she promised to never ever forgive me.

When the Old Man got home, he knew something was up. He beat it out of us without lifting a finger with his double down stare. He didn't really care about the things I'd broken in Big Sister's room, other people's pain never bothered him. When Big Sister leaned in for a sympathy hug, it made him snicker and say, "That's enough, now, you'll have bigger things to feel bad about later." He pushed her away and to get back at everything she pointed at me and said, "I caught him playing with my Raggedy Ann doll." The Old Man lit up. He gathered me in and went at it, "So now you're playing with dolls. How about we put you in a little dress and change your name to Suzy? What do you think all your friends and cousins are gonna think about that? Are you a goddamn sissy!? Huh? All the goddamn things I do for you around here and now you're gonna pull this kind of crap?" He pounded away at me. I ached to shut him up somehow, just a quick something, then run like hell.

One day I found the Old Man's Bowie knife hidden in a storage closet. The handle stuck out of an oily sleeve. I took it and put it under my pillow. I couldn't resist it. I lifted the pillow and studied the oily sleeve for awhile, then took hold of the handle and pulled it part way out. Seeing the blade made me shiver. I slid it back in, put the pillow in place and pressed my cheek against the top side. I could feel its outline. I began to daydream about stabbing the Old Man in his sleep. I'd wait for the setting sun and the boiled potatoes and chocolate pudding. I'd go to bed early after taking a second dessert and, when the Old Man clicked out the light, I'd take out the knife and squat in the hall, waiting for that horrible snore, that brutal sound. I'd creep to the door but that was as far as the dream would go. It wouldn't go any further. I knew I was doomed.

I got to playing around with the knife and ended up slicing open a finger and that was it for my weapon. The Mom bandaged me up and said, "Just wait until your dad gets home." I stalked off to my room and packed my little suitcase to go. While I was at it, the Old Man came home. I could feel his grumbling soul. I grabbed the suitcase and headed for the front door but he intercepted, mockingly, "Hey, Mick, where ya headed?"

"I'm running away."

"Is that right? Well, if you go, you can't take those new pants we bought ya. Let's take a look in the suitcase, see what ya got in there." He took possession, "Well lookey here." He pulled out Raggedy Ann, "You just can't keep from stealing can you? Where's the goddamn dress you should have packed?" He dug some more, "And you sure as hell can't take these shirts or these toys or any of this crap with you. They belong to me not you."

The Mom joined in, "That's right, you can only take what you paid for and you didn't pay for any of it and besides that suitcase belongs to your sister. You'll have to leave empty handed." The Old Man took over, "Maybe we can rig up a hobo outfit for ya since you'll probably be out riding the rails. We'll make you some sandwiches, wrap them in a handkerchief, and tie it to the end of a stick like they did in the old days."

They set me up and walked me to the door and told me to write often. I crossed the alley and hid in the cat lady's yard. It was very shady – the cats were well fed and friendly – the cat lady wasn't. A couple hours later, she spotted me and told me to get out of there. I stepped back inside in time for dinner. The Mom was making chocolate pudding for dessert. My sliced finger ached. Big Sister was coloring at the table. She seemed more agreeable. She let me watch over her shoulder. Best of all, the Old Man didn't seem to notice me at all...

The lunch whistle pulled me out of the lights and I headed to the break room to take a nap, but Brat had a couple joints and some blackberry brandy, so we hightailed it to his car. Bent came along just for the ride, or so he said. We were barely out of the parking lot when he worked himself straight and started wondering out loud when we were gonna smoke that joint. Brat found his begging hard to take, so he bent him back in place, "In a fucking minute, alright? You should have a sign around your neck that says 'get me stoned'."

Brat busied himself selecting the lunch hour music. Eventually, he pulled a joint from his wallet, "Hey, Mick, torch it and bring it back this way." I flicked and dragged and passed off to Brat, then, he took a hit and passed it back to me. I took another drag, sent a little wink to Bent in the backseat, and handed it over to Brat. At first Bent laughed it off, but as we continued back and forth, working our way to the roach, he tried to snatch it at the handoff. He knocked the cherry loose and it dropped and burned a hole in Brat's crappy suede seat. Brat came unglued and started swinging at the backseat. Bent angled into the rear window and snickered for forgiveness, "What's the big deal this car is fifteen years old, anyway, sorry." That wasn't good enough for Brat, he swerved the road trying to get Bent, the red cherry rolled between us, burning an ocean wave, a syncopated line, a hilarious story about some mixed up kids and their broken lives. I got hold of the rolling cherry and snuffed it out while Brat and Bent settled it like men with drinking problems. We rattled our way back to the plant.

Back on the job, we found that our condition was perfectly suited for working in a turkey plant. "A little extra meat on the floor never hurt anything. Clear it out of the way! Yo! Sweep it clean – we got turkey hams to make – a couple of those career girls aren't half bad – even Golden Retriever can lick my chin." We agreed that from then on we would get loaded every goddamn day.

A Packet of Ketchup

We parked the car in front of every bar in town, then twice more because we couldn't stop ourselves. We drove to the Burger King and went in for the usual stuff. We were the straw men but you couldn't tell us that. There was a pale girl with even paler eyes taking orders. We ran simultaneous covert surveillance on each other with tucked heads and roving eyes – up at the menu – down at the counter – up and over to catch a slice of her and, there she was catching a slice of me. By the time it was my turn to order I was all flustered and she was blushing and our pupils were expanding, threatening to swallow the universe. A mere counter and two thin strips of fabric between us, we pressed up against our sides and dream-walked together for as long as we could, but the line behind was stacking up from the long filing-in of the loud and louder – drunkards demanding special orders.

Later, she wandered by our plastic booth and wiped me down with a smile. My cheek to her thigh, the curve of it, I dove into my imitation chocolate shake. My roommates had zero tolerance for love that wasn't their own. They pulled me out of the booth, through the door, threw me in the car, we went home to our cots.

A couple nights later, it was back around the bar track two or three times more, then on to the Burger King and there she was again, but I was so far gone on bluesy booze it was enough just to be standing. I had thoughts of love, kindness, and understanding in there somewhere, but I didn't know how to get them out, let alone what I'd do after. I spotted a packet of ketchup on the counter and slammed my fist down on it, sending out a glob of red sugar paste that landed on her blouse. I grabbed a paper napkin and insisted on rubbing it in. She was not amused, even I could see that – love is fleeting.

I sat in the booth with my tray of crap, in a drunken fixation. I thought for sure she'd taken a piss in my coke or wiped my patty on her ass or spit on the fries. I sniffed at my food. I couldn't tell. The roommates played with me. They whispered in my ear all sorts of conspiracies involving her ass and my hamburger patty. They winked and chuckled and suggested that I do something about it. I agreed. I got up, staggered into range, threw the burger at the counter, screamed something in Japanese. I couldn't see her face, but I heard the door to her heart close with a clank, and instantly I was sad. I wanted to go back to the other night and get her number and be planning a night out with no counter or fabric between us. But then a new love suitor threw his drink in my face and everyone let out a cheer for the new hero. This emboldened New Love Suitor, suddenly he wanted to take it outside, "C'mon ya stupid drunk fucker, let's go." I'd had enough. I wiped down my face and bowed religiously back to my seat and the rest of my life.

The Turkey Plant II

We pushed the last of the turkey hams into the smoker. We looked each other over and couldn't help but laugh and laugh. Words were no longer useful, each one of us was worse than the last – no matter whose head was rolled, it turned up snake eyes.

True nature is a spiral we've hammered into a wheel, partly by choice, mostly by plated matter. Our wheel lies horizontal on the ground and we ride it like a merry-go-round at a million revolutions per hour. We hold on for life, not dear life, just life, and if there's a dream in there somewhere, we leave it be or get thrown in the gutter. "Stay to the middle, son, cling to the post." This is what it is to be working class poor.

I walked home from the turkey plant in the late afternoon, fifteen degrees outside, no wind, no clouds, no light. The anemic sun poked through just above the horizon. Down in the basement, Former Classmate was just getting his day started. He rubbed his eyes with the palms of his hands, stretched his arms above his head, sucked in the basement air, filtered out the dust mites, let loose a Moby Dick yawn, took a slow turn to me, "Fuckin' A, Mick, you look terrible."

I was ready for my cot, but there was a pizza on the way and a brand new bag of weed and water bong. What's the point anyway?

To decide? Which way? How much? What for? And this night, this gravelly night, just might be my last night on earth. I'll study in the next life, I won't plant any landmines, I'll steer clear of the graveyard, I'll stay out of the shadows.

The pizza and other roommates arrived on cue, as if by divine right and we were halfway through the box before it hit the wobbly table. We scarfed down slices, swigged the beers, passed the pipe – our burps and farts were intermingled. The party was dull so I grabbed a pint of tequila and chugged it down, all of it. I threatened mutiny and promised to beat the next face that appeared in front of me. I rammed my knuckles into the cinderblock walls as my roommates ducked out of the way, well in advance.

"Stop telegraphing your punches! A good fighter will beat the hell out of you." I could still hear the Old Man's words in my head as I bobbed and weaved like the old days, when the living room was squared off, and the Old Man brought out the sixteen ounce gloves (the Mom laced us up) and dispatched all my teary attempts to bring him down. He'd goad me from his corner between rounds, "I'm gonna stop going easy on you so you better keep your guard up." As he climbed out of his corner, I let loose a Hail Mary right hand shot and caught him on the chin. That's when the demon tore loose and he came at me with all he had for a full two minute round. He battered me down with red-eyed haymakers. Later, he let me know that it was my fault for making him blow.

I was punch-drunk and there was only one solution available at the time – I stumbled up the stairs, out the basement door and down the road, looking for the moon or Big Dipper. Former Classmate followed in his Pinto. He pulled up along side and tried to save me, "Mick, you stupid son of a bitch, get in before you freeze your ass off." I couldn't feel a thing. He tackled me to the ice, threw me in the Pinto, dropped me on my cot, set the alarm. It went off at five in the morning. I was still loaded, the cold wobble to work didn't help.

I arrived to find that the turkey ham machine was down for repair. They put me on the turkey and gravy line. A turkey and gravy guy gave me the low down, "Just line up ten boxes at a time edge to edge to edge, get a hand on both sides and squeeze them together tight so they don't slip, then whirl around like so and slide them onto this rolling rack, then spin back and line up ten more. Do that again and again and again until the morning break bell. Don't slack off on the pace because the overflow will clog the line and we don't want that."

The turkey and gravy line ramped up at 7:00 a.m. with sights and sounds of suckers and blowers and conveyors and funnels and inkers and rollers and flappers and spongers and blue collar girls. I stood at the end of the line watching the front edge of a tidal wave coming my way. It hit at 7:03 and by 7:04 my stomach was doing most of the work – sending cold sweat waves over my face – my mouth ran dry, filled to a gag, dried out again. I whirled and twirled like a lawn sprinkler spitting boxes of turkey and gravy in every direction. By 7:05 my gut was through sending warnings. I puked on ten million boxes of turkey and gravy. The blue collar girls on the other turkey lines looked, then looked away. It was too much even for them. I stumbled toward the bathroom, sidestepping the splatter. I puked every ten feet. When I reached a toilet I was all out of steam. I continued in a dry heave. My head throbbing, eyes burning, my face was tearstained. I asked myself, "Jesus Christ, Mick, you stupid son of a bitch, when are you gonna learn?" I was half bent retching up the last dried bits of my soul.

What a laugh. After all these years I'd finally run out of juice and there I was still heaving on a cold tile floor, just like where it began. I was a baby and the Mom set me on the tube sock rug and left me awhile to wheeze on my own. I sneezed and fell over, face forward. I sniveled in the fibers. Thirty pounds overweight, too much for me to overcome, but it made the Old Man proud, "How in the hell can powder and water cause this kind of weight gain?" He leaned over me, "It's a goddamn miracle! This kid is gonna be something. He's a goddamn bull elephant." The Mom nodded in agreement and smiled into my watery blue eyes. I blinked as hard as I could. She got the signal and bent down to scoop me up. The Old Man intercepted, "Leave him be will ya, you'll turn him into a goddamn sissy with all that goddamn cuddling." The Mom retreated to the couch and tried to seem encouraging, but her tiny weak smile couldn't bridge the gap. The Old Man was in between and it was gonna stay that way – I could feel it. It was as real as anything.

A few hours later the Mom picked me up and hugged me all the way down the hallway, but it was already too late. She put me to bed. I began to seep, spill and drain away through my eyes and nose and mouth and ears and dick and ass. I crusted over and almost suffocated in my crib. I sucked on tiny strands of air through hairline cracks. I couldn't get enough inside me to get out a good cry for help – it was enough just to survive the unblinking night. The next morning the Mom appeared and broke through the crust and wiped out the corners with a hot wet rag, lugged me down the hallway, put me on the couch, pulled up the tube sock rug and shook it out on the front step – like that was the problem – then slipped it back in place, stuck me in the middle and pointed me toward the flickering box and all its fuzzy happiness.

It took me all day to roll to the edge of the tube sock rug and stick out a puffy hand and feel the cold tile floor and love it for some reason. I pressed my cheek against it and fell asleep, exhausted.

I woke up when the Old Man slammed the front door. It must have been three years later. I was still draining away and crusting over and I still couldn't get to my feet or say anything beyond, "Cookie!" The Old Man wasn't happy. He stood over me as usual,

"What's with this goddamn kid – is he retarded?" He turned to the Mom, "For Christ sake, stop feeding him all that goddamn crap, he's wider than he is tall."

The Old Man pulled me by the heels off of the tube sock rug and onto the tile floor. He was always up to something. He stepped around, grabbed me by the wrists, hoisted me up, placed me on my feet and let go. I went down like a sack of rotten potatoes. Pus and mucous and shit and piss squeezed out of me. He tried several more times with the same results, then gave it up and left me lying in it. He moved to the recliner on other side of the room, lit a cigarette, and sat with his legs crossed at the knees staring at the flickering box. Big Sister wandered by and lorded over me until the Mom arrived with the mop, shooed her away, then cleaned the floor and me from the same bucket. The Old Man put it like this, "We gotta save every goddamn penny we can, there's no use buying two different kinds of soap." The Mom agreed, "It's good to save pennies."

The Old Man kept on dragging me to my feet and dropping me on the speckled tile. One day I caught hold of the edge of the couch, got a running start and never looked back. The stuff kept pouring out of me, though, and I shrank to my natural puny size. The Old Man was deeply disappointed. I kept moving. The Mom followed behind, at some distance, with the bucket and mop. I ran everywhere, around corners, into walls, knocked stuff over. I left behind a long running series of puddled disasters.

I experimented with crayons and the portable heater. In the bathroom, next to the toilet, there was a hardcover book with cowboys on the cover. I laid it in front of the portable heater and put a couple of my favorite crayons on the cowboys, then turned the knob as far as it would go. I wandered away with a new dream in my head and forgot about it until I heard the howls of the Old Man. There was something in there pushing him along. I didn't want to deal with either one of them. I dove for the floor and wiggled under my bed and refused to come out when he stormed into the room and threatened, "If I have to pull your ass out of there you're gonna get it much worse." I wasn't going anywhere. There was no difference between bad and worse when it came to the Old Man. He got to his knees – he hated doing that – reached under the bed, caught hold of my arm, dragged me through the bed frame and gave me a couple stings so I knew he meant business. He hauled me by the wrist to the side of the toilet, picked up his book and took a swipe at my head. Then he held it to my nose – my crayons had melted into his cowboys. It was the end of everything and he wanted to make sure I knew it. I told him I did, but it didn't matter now, things tend to see themselves through. I was beginning to see that...

After the dry heaves, I washed up, wiped my teary eyes, walked into the break room, grabbed my time card and punched out forever. I'd made up my mind I couldn't go back. The room was empty. I stammered in the middle and thought, I need something for them to remember me by besides a hallway full of puke. I ran over to the company fridge and took as many packages of turkey meat as would fit under my coat. I was stone cold sober by then. I ran out the back way – no plan as usual – headlong – out the door – clutching meat with elbows and hands – swing low, you working class maniac.

On the way back to the basement, my eyelids froze shut from the tears and the cold. I crawled the last couple of blocks, laughing, yes, laughing. I bumped my head against the basement door, it didn't sour me at all. I slid head-first down the stairs and nearly collided with the landlady, who was making her way up from the basement after collecting the rent and a quick snoop around. She wanted to talk about the water bong on the coffee table and the other three in the closet. I sailed right on past her yelling, "Gravity calls!" But that wasn't good enough for her because it was her basement so she scrambled down after.

I propped myself against the refrigerator while she poked me with the rent envelope, "When are you boys gonna cool it? I'm tired of hearing you guys at all hours like this and that thing over on the table, my word, I may have to call the police." I nodded in agreement. "Why are you nodding your head at me?"

"I'm just agreeing."

"Agreeing to what?"

"To whatever you're saying," I opened my coat, "Oh by the way I brought you a gift." I gathered up the turkey products and handed them to her before she could refuse. She held the meat and stammered, "Ah, well, then, so, you boys are really gonna need to cool it." I nodded in agreement. She continued, "Well, good then, I mean, I was young once too, you know. I don't wanna be hard on you boys. I suppose once in a while it would be okay." I kept on agreeing until she was out of sight.

I found my cot and fell in. Every cell in me hummed like a rust belt city in its heyday, pouring toxic waste over the surrounding area through the air – the stream – the lake – the open pit – the landfill. The landfill that will be re-zoned and re-graded for the next suburban dream along with the small print and plausible denial. So a cousin or two may be born with a withered hand, crooked legs, a loopy eye, something you'll never ever be allowed to talk about.

Former Classmate arrived with the afternoon sun. He banged on the basement window because he forgot his keys and, anyway, it was time to do something, anything, but this here thing right in front of us, "Come on let's go – it's the weekend – time for a road trip. Let's head to Mankato, you were born there right? I've got an aunt, uncle and cousin down there. You'll like my cousin, he really knows how to party. We can stay with them."

I arose from my cot, stiff like a mummy, and we beat it to his little blue Pinto with a bag full of goodies. It wouldn't start. I popped the hood, removed the air filter, flipped the butterfly and sprayed starter fluid directly into the carburetor while he turned it over. It kicked and coughed and flames shot out, then, a lone cylinder hit and dragged the other three along for the ride until one by one they sputtered to life.

Poor little Pinto died twice on the way out of town. "It takes forever for this thing to warm-up." We smoked some weed then Former Classmate was feeling drowsy and couldn't see very far down the road so I took over. I took highway 13 south out of Willmar. Former Classmate said, "Since I'm not driving, maybe I'll have a drink." He drank up half the bottle of brandy as the sun gave us a final wink and left us in the dark. Shortly thereafter, he did the same to me.

I flipped on the headlights, shaky in their sockets, they strobed the landscape. The road was bare with a wind kicking up out of the west. The snow was beginning to drift across the road in little grainy white whispers, such a barren time of the year. The moon dropped in for a while and confirmed that it was indeed a skeleton – the bones of Blue Earth County. I sang in my head as my eyes danced between the road – the mirror – the speedometer – the gas gauge – back to the road – to the mirror – a glance over at Former Classmate (out cold) – back to the road – to the driver's side mirror – shift in the seat – stretch the feet – back to the road – a gaping yawn – steer with a knee – stretch again – shake the head – glance at Former Classmate (still cold) – another yawn – eyes close – drift to the left – eyes open – straighten it out – to the mirror – to the speedometer – to the road – adjust the temp – to the road – turn up the stereo – back to the road.

Suddenly, the Pinto started to buck and snort and then it just quit. I rolled it to the shoulder and wound it over and over, there was nothing, not even a cough of encouragement. "Get up goddamn it we're stuck out in the middle of nowhere." Former Classmate grumbled to life. I pushed him out of the car. We stood with no hats, boots, gloves, and scanned the horizon for the nearest farmhouse. The closest one was at least a mile away. "Well, that's it then." I kept Former Classmate in front of me, pushed him along, "Come on man we ain't got all night." Less than hundred feet along Former Classmate stumbled over a short post in the ground that was marking something. He caught it with a shin and went down hard. I tried to help, "Get up, man, before you freeze to death." I offered a cold hand, he labored to his feet and rode his good side, "Dude, I can't make it, I can't make it, I gotta go back to the car."

"If anybody is going back to the car it'll be me. It was clear back when we started that something was wrong with that piece of crap, so you're going to make the trek with me. I'm gonna run back to the car and get the brandy. Wait the fuck here."

Every half step, Former Classmate would drink drink drink and by the time we got to the farmhouse he was a roman candle firing brandy cocktails from both ends. You could see him in the dark, in a light brown mist, giggling like he was swimming in fairy dust.

We knocked on the door, pleaded our case on the doorstep and were let in by the farmer's wife. Her kitchen was decked out in ears of corn. They were everywhere, lining the drapes, patterning the wall, magneting the fridge, peppering the linoleum. We stood in the middle and Former Classmate burped, farted and giggled, in short, he fairy dusted the corn. Farmer's Wife gave away a slight squint of annoyance in her eye but that was it, she didn't mention a thing about it. She leaned toward the dishtowels hanging in a loop next to the sink and recommended a call to her tow truck cousin who ran a part-time repair shop – usually worked late into the night to keep the farm afloat and, of course, we'd have to pay him cash. She got him on the phone and set it up, then pushed us out of the corn saying, "He'll meet you at the car. Good luck."

We zig zagged back to the Pinto. I zigged faster than Former Classmate zagged and soon he was lost in a dust cloud wandering the fields by himself. He stumbled around and got within twenty yards of the road once, before sitting in a row with the battered remains of last year's corn crop.

What a goddamn night! I sat in the Pinto smoking weed and dialing the radio. What did I care about going to Mankato anyway? The tow truck arrived and lit up the Pinto. Former Classmate stumbled up with a piss stain on the front of his pants, because he didn't pull it out in time, it was nearly frosted over. Tow Truck hauled us back to his shop and before Former Classmate's pants had dried, he found the problem, "The gas filter is plugged up." He held it up to the light, "She wasn't getting any gas. I'm seeing a lot of cheap auto parts these days. This isn't a genuine Ford gas filter, it's what they call an after-market gas filter. Looks like the real thing, but it's about a hundred times cheaper. These auto parts are causing a lot of problems out there, but I guess it's good for business."

Tow Truck screwed in a new filter and slipped the gas line back in place. I cranked it over and the Pinto jumped to life, then settled into its usual wobble. Tow Truck wrote up a repair receipt to make it official. "Let's see, that's forty for the tow and let's say twenty for the filter and labor. That'll be an even sixty dollars."

We arrived in Mankato. Former Classmate didn't know the difference. I couldn't shake him loose. I got us there and did he thank me? Not a word, it was all he could do to keep breathing. It took his uncle, cousin and I all we could handle to pull him out of his seat, he was a monster pussy cat. We could barely clear the ground with him, so bumped his ass along the way, then dropped him in the spare bed.

There was no need to hang around waiting for Former Classmate to wake up. His aunt and uncle were ready for bed anyway so I said, "See ya later," jumped in the Pinto and drove to the neighborhood (where I was born and bred) and parked outside the grandparent's old house. Someone else was living there. They probably tore out the basement bar. I looked up and down the street.

The big elm trees were gone, destroyed by same thing that will destroy us – a lack of depth and diversity. Everyone I knew from the old neighborhood had moved on or were dead. Nothing lasts in this fucking world except this bottomless sorrow. I reclined my bucket seat and turned off the heater. I wanted to feel the cold. I thought about my little country neighborhood up north and the neighbor kid who lived at the end of our dead end road, right next to the railroad tracks. As a kid, whenever I felt a train coming, I would jump on my dump-salvaged Schwinn one-speed bicycle, race up the driveway and down the lumpy asphalt to the end of our dead end road. Neighbor Kid would already be there, sipping a purple Shasta, trying to look unconcerned. We'd pick up chunks of iron ore and throw them at the sides of the cars and watch them burst against the steel hoppers, leaving a dull red blemish. When the caboose passed we'd stand at attention, then turn away and laugh and one of us would suggest a game of one-on-one basketball. I would get my own Shasta from Neighbor Kid's mom. She was so kind, gentle and worried – much older than the mom I knew. She was a painter, thin oil on thin canvas, scenic scenes mostly. One time she oiled up a painting of the Old Man's mini-ranch. It was a through-the-tamarack-gate perspective, with its set of elk antlers tacked tackily to the top, a long dirt driveway – the kind with a grassy center – a parallel of tamarack fencing, wind breaker trees, blue cloudy day striking brownish green, a crappy house, requisite propane tanks, crab apple trees. She made it appear somewhat idealistic – a leaning Rockwell but not quite. There was a dog, birds, wind, rustle, drab, but no people. I imagined myself inside the painting tearing up the place. She left us out. There was no way to make us look pretty. She knew the Old Man had a demon festering inside but, like a good old Midwestern mother, she kept it private. She took long walks with the Mom almost every night. The walks dragged on forever. I was always hungry so made a big fuss – they switched to after dinner. I didn't see the Mom again until the morning, at the stove, making pancakes, bacon and eggs in between sips of coffee...

I pulled up the next morning. Uncle greeted me at the door, "Did you sleep in the car?" "Yeah, something like that." I sat in the kitchen tapping my toes while Uncle was hard at a heroic tale, about himself, of course, and his mad swinging-at-everything days. First he was in a chopper, it was hit, he was in the air freefalling to the rice paddies below, spraying bullets with twin machine guns (no one's ever seen anything like it and never would again), took out at least thirty, broke his leg on landing – that's the only reason they caught him. It still took them three days to find him and, even then, he took out six more. He adjusted imaginary gold medals and hats with his Popeye forearms – he was proud of them, they were his best feature. He kept his sleeves rolled up just in case, but what could possibly happen anymore in Mankato? They hung the Indians and killed off the wildlife long ago.

Former Classmate limped into the kitchen. Uncle cleared a spot for him and said, "Good morning, Mary Sunshine, what makes you rise so soon? You know, you're one heavy son of a bitch. Dead weight, that's what you are, nothing heavier than dead weight. And Mick, here, is as weak as a girl so I had to carry you myself. I threw you over my shoulder, that's what I did, and took two steps at a time up the stairs. Ain't that right, Mick?"

"Hallelujah!"

Cousin dropped by the kitchen to say goodbye, "Sorry guys but I had a trip planned out of town." We decided to take our hangovers back to our basement. Former Classmate was still in no condition to drive. There was a winter sun and a stiff breeze out of the west with a temp around thirty-five degrees. The sun was unbearably bright, so low in the sky, it mirrored off the snow drifts and bare wet pavement – a double whammy. I pulled off and bought a five-dollar pair of sunglasses. That would do. "Now where is that joint?" I fingered the glove box. I poked at Former Classmate, "Wake up man! It's time for a smoke." He nodded his head then went back to sleep. Just as well, I liked the peace. I even snorted a little coke. I called it a chauffeur's fee.

Nothing matters when you're driving a car. As long as there is enough in the tank, the whole world can go to hell. It's our dream box on wheels. You don't age naturally in a car. A sixty-five-year-old in a loaded Benz can sprint with the young bucks. Time moves on, but you just stay there, pedal to the metal, the world is your oyster. Anything is still possible. When I turned fifteen, I got a farmer's license. I wasn't a farmer, but I thought, why not get a jump on things? The farmer's license allowed me to drive a vehicle, but only during daylight hours and within ten miles of home. I ignored both.

Big Sister got a '64 Ford Fairlane 500 from Gramps for her sixteenth birthday; two door, dark blue, with a 289 V8 and posi-traction. Big Sister went out one night with some friends and got loaded, so loaded her friends had to bring her home and carry her to the front door. The Old Man went ballistic. He threatened everybody but me. Big Sister giggled and cried and apologized, then puked in a bowl the Mom had provided. I was given de facto control of the Fairlane 500. She was grounded forever. I left the next morning. I was the only fifteen-year-old on the road. I basked in the glory of it. I attracted a party wherever I turned up the dust. I quit the bowling team.

An older kid didn't like the attention I was receiving. He drove a Buick Skylark with a 302 V8, but it didn't have posi-traction. I was leaving the bowling alley when Skylark cut me off at the door and challenged me to a drag race out on Cuyuna road. I'd come too far to say no, it was like he was challenging my very essence. Word got out and soon we were a caravan heading out of town. An ex-bowling buddy rode along with me. We sped to the racing spot, traded leads, took stupid chances. We arrived ahead of the rest.

Cuyuna road is a dark narrow strip with trees on the side. A perfect place for a deer to run out in front of you, but we didn't consider that. I rolled down the window and yelled to Skylark, "I'm gonna make sure the road is clear ahead." He yelled back, "I'm coming too!" And then, we were racing down Cuyuna road.

Ex-bowling buddy wasn't ready for it, he clung tight to the seat and door handle, clamped down on his tongue, struggled for his breath, "I don't know about this."

Skylark had some pep, my foot was to the floor, we rode side by side all the way to a long bend to the right. We barely let up and stayed side by side through the corner, then floored it again on the straight-a-way. We ate it up fast. The road bent back to the left. I was feeling lucky, I figured Skylark would hit the brakes at least a little bit. He was thinking the same thing about me. We careened around the corner, tight, like Latin dancers. It was all I could do to hold the road. Out of the corner, Skylark let off the gas – I saw my chance. I gunned the motor and flew past. In an instant we were in the tiny town of Cuyuna. It was dark. The headlights caught some kids riding their bikes in the street dead ahead. Ex-bowling buddy screamed, "Look out!" I hit the brakes and stabbed the wheel to the right – there was a corner and a baseball field. I missed the corner. Someone had planted four short posts to mark the boundary of the field. I missed three out of four, but the fourth one blew both tires on the driver's side. The forty pound metal glove box fell open and cracked ex-bowling buddy on the kneecaps. He wailed like a Blue's train while I limped the car off the field and swung around to the side. Skylark pulled up, "Holy shit! Did you see that!?"

"I was there wasn't I?"

The caravan arrived soon after. I was under fifty lights. I opened the trunk with a screwdriver and, behold, there were two spare tires. I changed the tires in the headlights while "Aqualung" played on a car stereo. Everyone was talking about how crazy I was.

Skylark filled in the details. He turned me into a danger seeking rebel. I let him go at it. I was busy trying to work out a plausible story I could give the Old Man regarding the two blown tires.

I got the tires changed. There was a Q & A, then, the caravan wandered away one or two cars at a time. Skylark and I were the last to leave the scene. It was ours after all.

I gave ex-bowling buddy a ride home. The car gave out a high pitched squeal. "What the hell is that?" I didn't know, he didn't care – he was still rubbing his knees. I screwed together a story about a railroad tie someone dropped in the road, around a corner, impossible to miss – I'm only fifteen!

I dropped ex-bowling buddy off in his driveway and he limped through his front door. I drove home, squealed down the driveway, went in, woke the Old Man (it was better to get him when he was groggy) and told him the railroad tie story. He grumbled and went back to sleep. I went to my room and curled at the edge of the bed and gave up everything. The dull buzz of billions of mosquitoes flapping their wings outside the window screen was the perfect reminder of what I had coming. Then like a shot it hit me. I knew why the car squealed the whole way home – the parking brake! I forgot to release the parking brake! I thought. I had to know. I slid open the window screen, damn the mosquitoes, jumped out and made my way to the Fairlane 500. I popped open the door and, sure enough, the parking brake was still set. At least that problem was solved…

When we arrived back at the basement, Former Classmate woke up in a foul mood – too much sleep from too much alcohol. We slid through the basement doorway and tore through the coke, just for the hell of it, and had the usual arguments and fistfights.

The party ended like always, on the morning of the worst hangover ever. I got up around two in the afternoon and stuffed my crap in a plastic garbage bag. The roommates were out running errands. We'd said our goodbyes the night before in a stoned, coked, drunken stupor. It was the only way we could communicate our true feelings. Of course, we wouldn't remember, but that was just as well. It was written on the puke-stained carpet.

I put my basement door key on the wobbly table, grabbed the garbage bag and made my way up the stairs as though I were held to the corners by elastic bands I knew were going to snap. I'll never climb these stairs again, I thought, maybe I should have hung on to my job at the turkey plant. Ah, there's no going back, especially to that mess, I'd never live it down. Another thing ending always made me feel sad and empty. Even when it was the end of something shitty. It tore me up inside, never to see again the people and things that had become so familiar, even after just a few months. Landlady, so all alone, shuffling the floor in her plastic slippers, always inviting us up for a cup of coffee and a chat about nothing. We never went. In our minds it was pure labor. What would be the point of idle chit-chat with an old lady? It never dawned on us that sometimes you just need another warm body at the same table.

I thought about Bent and Brat. What the hell would become of them? Not much, probably. All in all, they really didn't mind the turkey plant. If they could keep their habits in check they might just make retirement with a few stories to tell, then, death and all its empty promises.

The road home was icy and full of potholes. I hit every one and things shook loose and fell to the road and bounced up and down under the car before spitting out the back. I watched them in the rearview mirror, tumbling on the pavement, sliding toward the ditch: nuts, bolts, icicles, plastic, rubber and metal debris. I wasn't going back and I wouldn't slow down either. I said it out loud, "I'll strip it to the bones if I have to. As long as I can steer the motor, that's good enough for me." I was heading home again – to the goddamn mini-ranch, the Old Man and the chokecherry wine.

Working Conditions

Spring arrived as it usually does for me – bitter, angry, forsaken, sleepy, thin, uncertain. All my frozen ailments came back to life. I scratched my legs raw with short, jagged, bitten fingernails, while the Old Man fussed about, hunched at the shoulders, expressing his inalienable rights, insisting on a no-free-ride agenda. But the economy was in the toilet – a quick flush and that would be it.

One day, my old pal Country phoned over and read a job ad from the Brainerd daily paper, "Listen to this, dude. Earn up to five hundred dollars a week – new company – great potential – no experience necessary."

"Hey, that sounds like us."

We showed up at 8:00 a.m. sharp, along with fifty or sixty others. They stuffed us in a room and surrounded us with cheerleaders – guys in three piece suits doing the go-fight-win. Head cheerleader got things rolling, "Here's the deal folks, we want you to watch this short video about our company and then we'll get the application process going. Okay? Fantastic!" A cheerleader pressed play. A cheerleader hit the lights. Everything inside the box was "fantastic". A new age was upon us, a golden age, a paradigm shift, household products that will change everything, get in while its hot, a whole new way to financial independence because that's what you want. Well, it could be you. The last horn sounded, the last angel descended, a cheerleader hit the lights, a cheerleader pressed pause. The angel flickered in mid-flight on the idiot box. I stared at it with my sleepy eyes while they handed out the job applications. Then head cheerleader said, "We need thirty 'commission only' sales people and one $7.00 an hour part-time administrator." A collective groan went through the room. Nobody wanted to sell that shit. The cheerleaders were ready for it. Being from the big city, they naturally assumed their role as bringers of fire, matches for Jesus and rural parking lot towns. "Hey everybody this is the first day of the rest of your lives. This is scientifically proven. We're gonna work with you all the way. The smart ones among you will see that this is an outstanding opportunity to get in on the ground level."

I didn't know what I wanted I only knew that I didn't want this, this job, this pyramid scheme, this dead-end. I always sink to the lowest level the situation allows. I filled out my application:

Name: Ted Nugent aka "the Nuge"
Address: the Motor city ya dumbass!
Experience: Rocking my balls off – puking on your girlfriend

I slid it over to Country. He snicker-grinned, shook his head, under his breath, "You crazy son of a bitch." He went at his eraser, then took the great leap downward. His read:

Name: Geddy Lee
Address: Great White North
Experience: I'm today's Tom Sawyer I get high on you – with the space I invade I get by on you.

We drew dirty pictures and shared them with our neighbors. Soon there was a commotion, a snickering revolt. Head cheerleader cartwheeled over and took a glance. He was not amused. He dropped his pom poms, "If you guys can't take this seriously maybe you should just leave." He quickly addressed the others, "And that goes for everyone else. We're here to make money, lots and lots of money, and we want you to make lots of money. So anyone who is not going to take this seriously should get up and leave now." Nearly everyone wanted to leap up, run for the hills, the dark woods, the thick swamp, but they stayed put on the outside chance of getting the part-time administration position. I held no such hope. In fact, I held no hope at all. I got up first and pushed past the cheerleaders. Country was right behind.

We picked up one other hopeless applicant in our wake. He followed us out the door to the parking lot and came around front, peddling backwards. He was excited and wanted to have a smoke and talk about it. He mulled it over with indelicate words. It felt good to walk out on something that was false, even though he couldn't put his finger on it. It was sad to see someone so happy about so little. Where would this take him but to the next job interview? The next stand-there-and-take-it? The next stacked deck? He kept the ball rolling, "Hey, you fuckers want a beer?"

"Dude, it isn't even nine in the morning."

"Might as fucking well. I got a twelve pack in my cooler."

We shuffled over to his truck, sat on the tailgate and drank it all before nine-thirty. We waxed and waned about everything but the broken toilets – the crooked shelves – the empty pockets – the impending doom – the nuclear war – the dying fathers – the gray gray gray. When the beer was gone and we were done staring at our feet, we threw the last empty can on the pile, lifted the tailgate, said goodbye forever and went home for the summer.

Fall arrived like a snot-nosed kid. I headed to the Twin Cities and rode a relative's couch on the condition that I look for a job. The job ads were ninety percent employment agency listings. They took a cut, but gave no guarantees, "You must be available and by the phone every morning from seven to nine in case we need you to scamper on down to a warehouse and unload trucks or stack boxes. No guarantee they'll need you tomorrow, they might even let you go for the day just after lunch, or, keep you 'til midnight. It's their prerogative. Don't forget to smile and obey and leave a good impression. Remember, you represent our agency and if you want further employment, you'll do it this way. Any questions? Great! Welcome to the team and have a great day!"

All the jobs were crap. It was an uphill battle to get a dime more an hour. It wasn't long before I hit my end and all I wanted was a little revenge, a little satisfaction, from the fucking system.

"Good morning, Mick, how are you today?"

"I'm alright."

"Great! Listen, we've got a wonderful opportunity for you over at Blah Warehouses. They need someone to stack boxes for the day. Now, they don't pay as much as some of the other warehouses, but if you make a good impression, they might take you on full time. Then you can work your way up. Isn't that great?"

I gave it all I had, "Yeah, that sounds great."

"Great! It's in Roseville, can you get there in thirty minutes?"

"Of course, and thank you so very much."

I hung up the phone and the pit of my stomach turned. I tried to ignore it. "Ah, hell, I should just go." I put my jacket on three different times but I never got past the doorknob. Each time I held back, took a deeper breath, by then I was sleepy. I went back to bed. About two hours later the phone rang. After that, it rang every ten minutes. Around eleven I picked it up. It was Employment Agency, frantic, "Mick! Where have you been? We've been trying to reach you. Why aren't you at the warehouse!?"

"I'm so very, very, very sorry Employment Agency. I was nearly halfway there when a tire blew out and I spun out of control and went in the ditch."

"Oh my, are you all right?"

"Yes, yes, but I'm pretty shaken up about it. I just came in the door and I was just about to call you. Please give Blah Warehouses my sincerest apology."

"They're pretty pissed off right now, but I'll let them know the situation. Let me ask you this, can you make it out there this afternoon if they need you?"

"Absolutely. I'd love to make it up to them."

A short while later, Employment Agency was back on the phone, "Hello, Mick, I was just in touch with the manager down there and he said they can definitely use you this afternoon. How quickly can you get there?"

"I'll leave right away."

"Great! I'll let them know you're on the way."

This time I only put my jacket on once, didn't go near the door, my blind resolve had deepened. I stood in front of the bathroom mirror and stared, "What are you doing to yourself?" I took the phone off the hook, made a sandwich, cracked one of Relative's beers and turned on the tube. Around four in the afternoon I hung up the phone. It rang almost immediately. I was ready. I answered with the low sad voice. It was Employment Agency, of course. "Mick! What the hell!? Why aren't you down at Blah Warehouses!?"

"I know, I know, but when I was about to leave I got a call from my mother. My poor sweet father had a heart attack and died. I've been on the phone this whole time trying to console her. She's very sensitive – I don't like to see her suffer."

"Oh, I'm so sorry to hear that. How are you holding up?"

"I'm doing okay. My father and I were very close, he was also my best friend."

"That's nice, listen, regarding Blah Warehouses, I'd really hate for you to miss this opportunity."

"I know what you mean, they sound like a great outfit."

"Do you think you might be able to work the nightshift this evening? They really need somebody to stack those boxes, it might do you some good, you know, keep your mind off things and still get the chance to make a good impression on the manager."

"Yes, you're right, stacking boxes would do me good right now. Tell him I'm on my way."

"Great! keep your chin up, kid, you'll get through this and it'll only make you stronger."

I drank a couple more beers and gave my old pal Country a call. He was living over by the University of Minnesota. We met up and put away a few pitchers of beer in some Dinkytown bar.

"I'm suppose to be stacking boxes right now. Ha ha ha."

"No shit?"

"Yep."

"Mick, ya stupid son of a bitch, what are you gonna do now?"

"I don't know, maybe I'll go to the University."

Next morning, Relative greeted my headache with the phone. It was Employment Agency absolutely livid, "Damn it, Mick, I know you're having problems, but if you say you're going to be somewhere for work, you need to be there and do your very best."

"I'm sorry. Yesterday was such a bad day. Right when I was leaving, I took a valium and drank a beer and passed out. I'm such a lightweight. Anyway, I just want to forget it. Please, is there anything available today?"

"Well, I don't know, maybe you should take some time off."

"No, no, no, the funeral isn't until next week and I really need the money to help pay for the tombstone."

"Let me take a look at the schedule. Hmm, have you ever operated a forklift?"

A lucky break! I'd always wanted to drive a forklift. Suddenly I could see myself putting in thirty soft years, easy money, climb the ladder, "Yes, I know it like the back of my hand."

"Okay then, I've got a three day stint over at the Blatz plant stacking crates. It pays twelve dollars an hour."

"Sounds great, what time do they need me?"

"Nine a.m. sharp. Don't mess this up, Mick, I'm taking on chance on you for this one."

"Awesome. I'll get there ten minutes early."

By eight-fifteen I was in another funk. The pit had turned once more. To go or not to go?

I showed up about ten minutes late. A grumpy manager let me in, looked me over, let out a long sigh and led me to the back of the warehouse. It was a big place – all lights, tin, concrete, stacks of crates, and twenty-some-odd forklifts picking them up and putting them down. It didn't make any sense. Manager handed me a clipboard with some work orders attached. "You know what you're doing, right?"

I was ready to fake my way forward, "You bet." He pointed me to my forklift and stood there while I climbed aboard. I acted like I knew what I was doing, made little make-believe adjustments to the seat and steering wheel. I figured how hard could it be? Just needed a little time to get acquainted. Luckily, the big squawking one-way speaker called for Manager and he quickly went away (everybody's got a boss). I got the forklift moving and I figured out the lift, but the rear-steering kind of threw me. The other fork lifters tried to zip back and forth, but I was in the way. They were not buying me as a fellow fork lifter. They honked and screamed, "Get the fuck out of the way, retard."

That was it, they wanted retard, so I gave them retard. I began to move at ten times the speed of safety. I left smashed crates in the aisles like broken eggs for Paul Bunyan. I stabbed at them with the forklift. I yelled at the fork lifters "Whaa-hooooo! I'm a communist! Let's form a Union!" One of the husky fork lifters jumped in front of me and demanded that I climb out of there. I climbed down and met up with him. I gave him the dull eye, "Sorry man, I guess I'm a little rusty."

"You fuckin' guess you're a little rusty? You need to stay off that fuckin' thing 'til Manager gets down here."

"No problem."

I put on my best stupid grin. Husky Fork Lifter didn't quite know what to make of me. I didn't give him time to make up his mind, "I'll go find, Manager, myself." As long as I was out of the way he didn't care. I left through the nearest exit and laughed and laughed and laughed. All the way to my rusty bucket of bolts and my one hundred ten dollar net worth, I laughed like an idiot. It felt so delightful to fuck that shit up. The poor bastards needed a story. They'll laugh about it themselves for weeks, months, years.

Maybe Husky Fork Lifter will give it a mention at his retirement party and he and his fellow fork lifters can chuckle together one last time, "It must have been thirty years ago when this retard son of a bitch got through the front door somehow and jumped on a forklift and tried to help." He'll wink at the other fork lifters and the chuckling will begin. "Well, let me tell ya, that cocksucker was dumping crates right and left. By God, he was causing thousands of dollars in damage." The fork lifters will nod in agreement and chuckle some more. "He was a whoopin' and a hollerin' and whatnot. Well, I cut him off quick and I was ready to kick the living shit out of him, but then he looked at me with that retarded grin and I just couldn't do it. That stupid son of a bitch had problems even I couldn't knock out of him."

Living Arrangements

I rented a two bedroom attic for the summer in Bloomington. An old high school chum set it up. He was already spending his fall, winter, spring at St. Olaf College in Northfield. The attic belonged to the parents of one of St. Olaf's football teammates and he lived there as well, on the main floor, the caretaker, a neat freak Adonis. His job was to police the premises for his missionary parents. His girlfriend helped, but only during daylight hours. She was fresh out of high school, an all-American bathing beauty. They were rabid Christians, scared to death of the world, no TV, no radio, no nothing. They sat around reading the bible, but not too close. They were saving themselves for each other.

They came to regard me as the devil upstairs. I was in a nasty state – wide awake. St. Olaf had to be diplomatic for the sake of the team. I counter-balanced by jacking off in the shower. I'd imagine Bathing Beauty in there with me. Such innocent conformity drove me mad with desire and disgust. Anyway, I refused to clean my mess. The attic became a pit. Neat Freak wasn't happy and would have squashed me, but I beat him to it.

I caught him in the kitchen one morning pushing some noodles down the drain. "Oh, lord, I'm so depressed. Oh what a mess I've made of my life. I'm sure I've lost Jesus and I feel I won't live much longer." Neat Freak saw an opportunity to save a little lamb. He brought me pamphlets with quotes from the bible. He cleaned up my mess while I studied the pamphlets with Bathing Beauty. I sat close, with a hard-on, staring at her intently, drilling my twisted thoughts into her head. I thought I could see a spark of something coming through her eyes, but I wouldn't bet on it.

St. Olaf worked a ditch digging job in Burnsville. He put in twelve hour days and when he got home, Neat Freak pinned him down in the kitchen, "I had to push some noodles of yours down the drain this morning. Please make sure it doesn't happen again." St. Olaf apologized over and over, all the way up the stairs. Soon enough it wore him thin, "This guy's intolerable, let's find another place to hunker down in."

We found a month-to-month in a generic complex, the kind with a crappy workout room and an outdoor pool that spent most of the year empty. The apartments were stacked three high. Each one had a small balcony with a sliding door, crappy gray wall to wall carpet, a strip of linoleum in the kitchen and bathroom, two shitty bedrooms.

We threw a kegger the first weekend and everybody showed up, including a few I didn't like. We didn't have any furniture so we packed them in tight. We were on the top floor, everything reverberated downward. The yard was mostly concrete and, man, did our shit carry. The cops knocked on our door every thirty minutes, luckily, a different set each time. So we got nothing but first warnings.

A dude showed up whom I hated for some reason. He was a gangly doofus with a flappy jaw, that was about it, not much to hate, but I hated him anyway. I gathered my small ring of drunks and shared my opinion of Doofus. Someone proposed that we do something about him, "We can't have him fucking up the party." A vague plan formed around the idea of dangling him upside down from the balcony. This required us to act friendly towards him to gain his trust, but of course we over did it and immediately put him on edge. We surrounded him with big cheers and backslaps and shots of tequila. We led him on a raid of the swimming pool area and came back with floatation rings and plastic chairs. We celebrated our victory with more shots and more cheers. One of my drunks coaxed him to the balcony rail and, seeing poor Doofus on the balcony, flapping his jaw so fucking helpless to the future, made me sad and the hate I'd stuffed him full of disappeared. That wasn't true for my ring of drunks. As soon as I hesitated, they were there to see me through, "Hey, Mick, come on, here's your chance." They waved me forward with glossy eyes, "Go for it man, don't be such a fucking pussy." I require the best of both worlds for my overall wellbeing. I fake bum-rushed Doofus, even pretended to stumble as I reached for his legs, thus giving him enough warning to make an escape. Which he did, out the door, up the hall, down the stairs in two, three, four concrete steps, then to his car in the parking lot and down the road. The cops showed up a little while later, spotted the pool furniture and shut us down.

I got Doofus on the phone a few days later and did my best to smooth everything over, "Hey, Doofus, about the other night, we were just fucking around with you and it got out of control. Sorry about that."

"Yeah, whatever. Hey, guess how many women my big brother has fucked?"

"I don't know man."

"Just guess!"

"Twenty."

"Twenty! Are you a moron? I've fucked at least thirty. Hey, did you know that I stay hard after I come? The ladies love it 'cause I can go all night."

Now I remembered why I hated Doofus in the first place. I wanted to go back to the other night and dangle him for real.

St. Olaf's girlfriend from school moved into the apartment with her purse full of compact mirrors. They met spring quarter in the dorm laundry room. Now, she was pregnant. The afflicted families got together and negotiated a settlement. St. Olaf and Spring Quarter were married in a one hundred-ten degree church. It was mid-August, I was best man, they were doomed. We stood there sweating in three piece suits, dripping with despair. They giggled through the ceremony but that didn't mean they were happy. It was that or get the hell out of there. The weight of their families kept them in place. They giggled for the end to come quickly.

They honeymooned in the parking lot while I moved the rest of her crap into the apartment. St. Olaf was depressed by the following Monday. By Tuesday he was staying out late. Sometimes he would just sit in his car and wait. He left it running in neutral and prayed, "Dear Lord, I'm here because the devil has had his way with me. I will fight the devil, Lord. I believe he is real and I will fight him Lord."

Whenever I stopped by for a quick change, St. Olaf was in the parking lot wrestling with the devil. He tried to bring me into the ring with him, "Hey, Mick, I want you to know that the devil is real and trying to destroy the world."

"Dude, I don't believe in the devil. People make their own choices in life."

"That's exactly what the devil wants you to believe."

He had me there, "I'd love to read the pamphlet."

Spring Quarter was frantic about St. Olaf's epic battle. She tried to give me her lifeless story. I offered little sympathy, "I'm sorry to hear that, but I have to go. You'll have to work it out with him."

Autumn rode in on an icicle and they went back to school –
rented a little house off campus – she stayed home with the baby – he
blew out a knee and stopped playing football – they left when he
graduated. The devil went along for the ride. It was a lifelong
commitment.

I rented another two bedroom apartment, this time with my
old pal Country. It was transition housing, some were going up, more
were coming down. We sat on the bottom floor with the wife beaters
and alcoholics. The screaming began every night around nine o'clock
and continued until everyone was thoroughly beaten, including us.
The rage and violence went right through the walls and infected
everything. Even the cockroaches were angry. They refused to
scamper away in the light, they stood their ground and wagged their
asses at us.

We threw a party one Saturday night and our crowd of casual
users straggled in for an evening of drinking games. By ten, everyone
was holding a grudge against everyone else. A trio of demons banged
on the door, then let themselves in – two guys and a girl. The guys
were twin pushers. Side by side they'd get you into a corner, then one
of them would insist he'd seen you before and that you had insulted
him. I crab-walked the room with a bottle of Moosehead. I kept them
in front, close to my pinchers. They made their way to the bathroom
and smashed the mirror and tore the door off the medicine cabinet
hoping to cause a stir, but it didn't bother me. I leaned against the
wall and blended in. The girl, on the other hand, was a seductress. As
the twins were pushing you around, she was pulling you in with a
two ounce test line. After the twins had vacated the bathroom,
Seductress reeled me in and while we stood over the mess, she
offered her sincerest apology and I accepted. Suddenly the twins were
back for another round and there I was leaning into Seductress. They
had me backed against the toilet. One of the demons spoke up, "Hey,
you stupid son of a bitch, she happens to be my girlfriend." I tried to
deflect them with a feeble, "Hey man, we were just talking." They

kept moving in. I changed tactics. "Hey, you assholes fucked up my bathroom and you're gonna have to pay for it!" That caught them by surprise. They assumed they would beat me in my groveling state. It gave me just enough room to force my way between them and get through the bathroom door. I yelled for Country, but he was busy drinking. My bedroom door was right next to the bathroom. I slipped through before the demons could re-assemble and twisty locked the door, then pushed the dresser in front of it. I opened the window and crawled through as the demons snapped the lock and pushed against the dresser. I got to my car, jumped in, reclined the seat and played dead drunk. Ten minutes later Country came tapping on the window with the demons in tow. "Hey, Mick, these guys were just fucking around with you. We've been knocking down shots together and they want to drink with you – come on."

"Yeah, I know I was just out here getting a little shut eye. It's so fucking loud in there." They weren't buying it, but I stuck to it religiously even though they kept bringing it up over and over, "Yeah, we really scared the shit out of you, man. You're a fucking pussy."

"Oh please, I knew it all along, someone's got to keep things interesting around here."

We poured shots of tequila into the wee wee hours. Most of the wife beaters were snoring by then. In the morning, the new marks on the cheeks and walls would be artifacts, ancient history for them. The semi-sorry wife beaters would complain, "Why do you want to go back there? The point is, woman, I'm human. I can change if you just give me a chance. You know I love you, but you know you can't say those kind of things to me. It sets me off. You should know that by now. Now, let's forget about it. Make me some breakfast."

A couple of the lower apartments still had a little life left in them. Out of one of them came the skankiest little woman of all time. She was, maybe, thirty-five years old, an eighty pound piece of beef jerky wrapped in a thin blanket. She pushed open our door and cried for help. She led us across the hall to her apartment. There was a short, fat, naked man standing in the living room and she wanted him out. He begged for some clothes. Country threw him a rug from the bathroom floor, "Here wrap yourself in this and get the fuck out."

At first, Skankiest was grateful. She followed us back to our place and helped herself to our booze. Then, she got so sad because she missed her abuser and he wasn't so bad when he was fully clothed. In my drunken haze I thought to myself, I'll pull off her blanket and bend her over the bathroom sink. "Turn on the faucet, dear, I'm tired of your whimpering."

Skankiest would never have made my girl list back when I was thirteen and retired to my broken down bed. I curled at the edge to avoid the rusty spring that poked through the mattress. I faced the wall, unrolled my girl list and tacked it in place over the snot stains on a pale blue wall. How many girls? I don't know, the number went up and down. They hopped on and off according to my whim. I was so far from being with any one of them, every night, before I fell asleep, I'd imagine myself saving all of them from some catastrophe, some unfortunate doom. The entire list would be trapped together in a pit. Whatever enemy was quickly dispatched, that wasn't the point, I was all about the after-party in the pit. The list would gather around adoringly, it was a mystery to them why they hadn't noticed me before this. I could have any one of them but I could never decide. I'd lift them out of the pit one at a time. Hold them close. Let them go. It only made them want me more. I wrote their names in flashlight then traced them over and over. My favorites were traced hundreds of times. They built up a lead base. They intruded into other girl's space. The intruded-upon would be erased and written out again further down the list. "It's a chance for us to get reacquainted," I would say. She'd pout and exclaim, "Oh the indignity!" I'd try to soothe her with, "Look how beautifully I'm writing out your name again. The way I curl your "y" I love the way you sit in class almost looking at me, your legs wrapped to the side, I can barely make you out. Your fuzzy outline only adds to your charm. I can promise you that I won't ever move you again but, we both know the nature of love. I just noticed that you're right under Brenda. She's new, but coming on strong." The flashlight began to fade, "Fucking alkaline batteries!" I rolled up my girl list and went to sleep.

SPIFF Incorporated

1.

I got a job as an office clerk. I was at the bottom of another chain. I was hired to do the filing, account receivables and the typing of a 3-carbon-copy company invoice for every high-pressure handwritten order turned in by the mustached sales staff. I made the rounds twice a day to collect their handwritten orders. It was like a parade. I broke up the monotony of their telemarketing careers by merely arriving – any excuse to get off the phone sufficed. They gathered around with coffee stained neckties and moustaches twitching and followed me from desk to desk, yucking it up or giving last minute details regarding their most recent high-pressure order.

"Hey, Mick, what's old, cold and sold?"

"I don't know."

"Yer momma!" They howled with laughter.

"I don't get it."

"You're not suppose to get it. It's just funny to say, 'Yer momma!'"

They rolled in the aisles and then one of them picked himself up off the floor, "Hey, Mick, let me see that order I just gave you." I shuffled through the handwritten orders while Moustache leaned over me. He spotted his order first, "Oh there it is. Now look here, Mick," pointing a sticky finger at a line of his scribble, "these here gas filters – the 229s and 332s – must go out no later than tomorrow. Can you promise me they'll go out by tomorrow?"

I gave him the company line, "All the parts go out the next day unless they are backordered and then we'll let you know."

"Okay, Mick, fantastic, yer the best. Say, what's old, cold and sold?"

"I think I've heard that one before."

"Yeah, I know a better punch line. It's funny as hell."

"Alright, let's hear it."

"Yer momma!"

They gathered for one more round of laughs and backslaps and high-fives and I returned to my post and mucked up the invoices on an IBM Selectric with a hunt – peck – miss – backspace, that was turning heads. "Can this guy even type?" Even the moustaches thought I wouldn't last, but I hung in there. Worked an extra hour each day to get the job done and smiled, never stopped smiling, "I'm a little rusty."

Timmy Tatters was the office manager. He was just a little further up the chain. "Hey, Mick, I was thinking that you might be able to, or in fact, know of a circumstance, whereby I might score some pot."

"Why me? Do I have a sign around my neck that says I know a drug dealer?"

"Oh, no, no, no, of course not. I just thought you were cool with that sort of thing."

"Yeah, I can probably help you with that."

Timmy Tatters was a good guy. He'd spent a few years in a seminary trying to will himself to priesthood. He was goodhearted, soft and eager to please and always looking for some grass for whenever he was stressed. He was always stressed. Smoking too much pot gave him asthma. He was okay with the trade.

SPIFF Incorporated was a boiler-room operation dug into a hill in Bloomington. It was a concrete shell with offices in front and a warehouse in back. They sold defective auto parts nationwide via the telephone. They boxed them to look genuine GM, then sold them at retail to the auto parts managers at new car dealerships all across the country. The only way to get the parts managers to take the crappy parts was to offer some sort of incentive.

It was up to the staff of high pressure moustaches to find out what that incentive might be and work them over, "Hey Parts Manager, this is Moustache calling from SPIFF Incorporated, how's it hangin' today? Good, good. Listen, Parts Manager, are you a hunter? Not anymore huh? You still like guns though, don't ya? Yeah, yeah, listen, Parts Manager, the boss just handed me a hell of a deal, now listen to this, go with me on just two gross of your best moving gas filters and we'll send you a brand new 357 magnum pistol absolutely free. That ought a put a little skip in your step today, eh, Parts Manager? Alright, so you're not much of a gun person, but I'll bet you love to shop, right? Everybody loves to shop! Tell you what, go with me on those same two gross of filters and I'll send you a two hundred dollar Sears gift certificate absolutely free – just my way of saying thanks. Yup, just two gross. Hey, what's your home address so I can send ya the gift certificate? Christmas is right around the corner, that two hundred dollar gift certificate would go a long way, wouldn't it? Maybe get your wife something special. Oh, you're not married. Well, have you got a girlfriend? How long have you been going out? That's fan-tas-tic! Let me ask you this, what're your best moving gas filters? Oh, the 230s and 231s, that's fan-tas-tic! Tell you what, go with me on a gross each of the 230s, 231s and a case of your favorite sparkplugs, and I'll send you a beautiful quarter carat diamond necklace absolutely free. What do ya mean how can we do it? It's just my way of saying thanks. Christmas is coming and the boss is in a great mood. This is only good today, right now. What do ya say, Parts Manager? Hello... Hello... Arrgh, the cocksucker hung up on me."

When they did get a parts manager to take a bribe they rode him hard to the grave. Every week, when Moustache needed to hit his quota, Parts Manager would have to give, usually under protest, "Listen, Moustache, I've got parts up the ying yang here, my hands are tied on this one. The owner has cut me off." Moustache would screw him down tight, "Does the boss know about the fucking ATV we sent you on his dime? Don't fuck with me here. All you need to take today is three gross of your favorite fucking filters and you'll be getting a top of the line Panasonic VCR."

The Moustaches were interchangeable. They popped pills, smoked like fiends, slugged away coffee by the gallon (three pots going simultaneously all day long) and everything was fan-tas-tic. With great big nicotine and coffee stained teeth, "I'm fan-tas-tic, but I'm getting better."

The top moustache was a vulture to the core. He wore a hand wrapped greasy cowboy hat, bolo tie, embroidered cowboy shirt, brown nylon pants, square toed boots. He only drove American, had a bumper sticker that swore to that fact. He was in his prime, sales wise. When that morning bell rang, he dove in and stayed head down, a low-intensity high-pressure beam, like he was dredging a hillside. He had them hypnotized. He could be in the middle of a sales pitch, have Parts Manager right by the nose, realize he had to piss, put him on hold, slam the phone down, do his business, grab another cup of joe, even yuk it up with the sales manager, before he got back on the blower. Parts Manager would still be there, hanging on the end of the line. "Alright where were we? That's ten pair of the 0212 CV joints and boots, and twelve gross of filters across the board.

And this time I get the prize because I do enough for you. Don't turn pussy on me, I'll come down there and cut your fucking throat."

Except for a core group of six guys, the commission-only sales position at SPIFF Incorporated was a revolving door of recent grads, sleaze bags, on-the-way-downers, drug addicts and con artists. They ran a continual ad in the local paper looking for one in a million.

They were always having team meetings. The chief moustache would walk in with a handful of daily, weekly, monthly, sales targets and say, "Hello gentlemen, whoever of you can move X amount by the end of today are gonna party tonight on my yacht on Lake Minnetonka." A collective display. "If we move such and such by the end of the week, I'm taking you out on Friday – dinner on me." Another collective display. "And one more thing, gentlemen, if we do a million this month, I'm taking you skiing in Aspen." An over-the-top collective display. Chief Moustache knew how to get them jacked up. Then he'd have the audacity – "Gentlemen, let us pray." He was a deacon in his church and he had a mistress to go with a wife and two kids. "Dear Lord, we hope and pray that this month will be profitable for everyone, especially me. Amen." A collective rising. After the handshakes and backslaps, it was back on the phone to shake them down. Look out Aspen, here they come, the bottom of the barrel with fists full of money.

I went out drinking with the moustaches a couple times. They were out of control. All that coffee and alcohol, those barbiturates and the high pressure lying, were taking a toll – eight to twelve screamers racing to the hole. They wore me out just standing next to them. They competed with each other at all things and every level with acid tongues and measuring sticks. "Hey, Tiny Moustache, how many times have you been divorced?"

"Why, I do believe I hold the record for this here office at three."

"Ha! Put me down for four."

"Bullshit! Show me all your divorce decrees."

"I will when you pay me the twenty dollars you owe me from last weekend's poker night."

"What!? I paid for your drinks the week before at the strip club – go fuck yerself."

They all had broken marriages and alimony and car payments and house mortgages and dogs and cats and five hundred gallon exotic fish tanks and a TV in every room and all the latest gadgets, hair replacement methods, a twice used Bo-Flex in the basement, a speed boat for when they went to their time-share, and various collections: football, baseball, hockey, basketball, stamps, coins, civil war shit, muskets, pistols, buttons, pussy, beer cans, tools, cars, motorcycles, playboy magazines, salt and pepper shakers, venereal diseases.

2.

I developed a personal grudge against SPIFF Incorporated. I voiced my displeasure to Timmy Tatters, "You know, just this past winter, I was stranded in a blizzard because of an after-market gas filter that probably came from this fucking company."

"Really? What happened?"

"I was driving my car with a friend when the cheap gas filter failed and left us stranded miles from anywhere. We had to hoof-it through the blizzard. I cracked my shin on a post. I almost lost my friend."

"Jesus, that sounds terrible."

"Yeah, it was bad."

"I can't say that I'm glad we do what we do, but, hey, it's a job."

"So Chief Moustache pays you pretty well then?" Our hippie girl receptionist, who usually sat smiling in a stoned silence, let out a little snort and said, "That'll be the day." Timmy snickered and with a nasal whine, "I'm not going to say how much I make, but I hired and trained the Office Manager who is now working over at SPIFF 2 Incorporated and she's already making more money than me."

Right next to Chief Moustache's office was a rather large walk-in closet space where he kept the guns (he was a licensed gun dealer), the video cameras, the Sears gift certificates and everything else SPIFF Incorporated used to generate the sales. They shipped them all over the country as soon as the mucked up invoice was paid in full. Chief Moustache kept the door double locked and only he and Timmy had a key. Said Timmy, "You know, he trusts me more than he trusts himself."

Once or twice a week, some parts manager, somewhere, would get to feeling guilty and return his prize. It was Timmy's job to handle the returned item. I made it a point to lend a hand. "Hey, Timmy, it seems to me that video camera is already paid for, why don't you take it home and put it to good use?" Timmy played along, "Maybe I will. Yeah, why not? I've got a cousin who's getting married next month. Maybe I'll give it to them as a wedding present, you know, save myself some bucks." I pushed some more, "Why not? That's a nice video camera. With what Chief Moustache pays you, you'll never be able to afford one." Timmy put the camera back in the closet.

Timmy was a rock but he wasn't granite. I became a water drop and kept at it, "Just look at this company bribing and then blackmailing these parts managers. What's so bad about taking a couple prizes? The moustaches are making a fortune, not to mention Chief Moustache and his little mistress, and the shit wage he pays us.

And I was left by the side of the road and almost died because of these shitty auto parts – this is personal." Timmy crinkled his nose. I threw him the sales pitch, "Listen, Timmy, a two hundred dollar Sears gift certificate was returned today and the boss says I gotta move it. Tell you what I'm gonna do, now hear me out here, Timmy. I want you to take this gift certificate down to Sears and pick out a brand new grill or tool set or bed spread or whatever else your heart desires – as long as Sears provides it. You like to shop don't you, Timmy? Everybody loves to shop. Maybe you should get a present for your new girlfriend. She deserves something nice for being so faithful. When has anyone ever done anything for you? Don't you deserve a little something? And it's free, free, free."

You can't talk anybody into anything. All you can do is help release what's already inside. A little slit and Timmy tore himself open. Soon enough, all returned merchandise was subject to redistribution, usually after 7:00 p.m. when the coffee pots were empty, the last of the phony orders were submitted and our receptionist was safe in the crisper at home. "Hey, Mick, did you get a video camera yet?"

"Yep, but I can always use another one."

"Well, here you go then." He handed over the camera and dug for some more. "Lookey here, another Sears gift certificate."

"How much?"

"One hundred dollars. I'd take it, but I can't think of anything else I need. I've got every damn tool they make."

"Yeah, I know what you mean, but here's a little trick I picked up last week. It happened by accident when I tried to buy a basketball with a two-hundred dollar gift certificate. Well, they didn't have enough change in the till so they sent me to customer service to cash it. Once they gave me the cash, there was no point in getting the ball so I left with the full two hundred. From now on, I'm going directly to customer service with the same song and dance."

Timmy was pleased, "Then I guess I'll take it."

I was pulling in an extra five to eight hundred dollars a month, depending on how many guilt ridden parts managers had started their twelve steps. Now, the fucking job actually paid a living wage. Chief Moustache could have saved us the trouble by paying us straight out instead of making us get it the way he did. But I forgave him, probably put it on video tape, or whispered it on the way out of Sears, or grinned it to myself after so many beers – giggling in that fucked-up sort-of-way I get when I'm about to reveal something super secret to the drunk the next stool over.

3.

One day, a bolt of lightning shot out of the clear blue sky and hit the SPIFF Incorporated company sign. There was a flash of light and a sound like the crack of a long metal lash snapping some ass. It blew chunks of brick and mortar all over the cars in the parking lot. It was after three in the afternoon, so I was half asleep, at my desk typing it up for the moustaches, listening to the office play-by-play as broadcast by Timmy Tatters.

With his nasal little voice he was the perfect AM radio. Like the days when I'd fetch a beer for Gramps and we'd sit together on the concrete slab – in the muggy sun – a broken robin's egg – the petrified grass – walnuts on the ground – my sliced and bruised bare feet – the tobacco stained radio tuned to 830 AM WCCO, broadcasting something wholesome – a baseball game, "Ladies and Gentlemen, have we've got a game going today. It's two out in the ninth, there's a man on first, and here comes Your Choice to the plate. It's a beautiful day here in the Twin Cities. Oops, looks like they're gonna talk about it. Catcher is running to the mound. There's a lot riding on this so they want to get it right."

"That's right, Halsy, Catcher is probably gonna remind Pitcher not to throw the high heat because that is what Your Choice would love to see. I'm sure they'll keep it low and away and mix in a couple of his big looping curve balls."

"Folks, the good people at Lindahl Oldsmobile would like to invite you to come on down this Sunday. That's tomorrow, folks. It's family day down at Lindahl Oldsmobile so bring the kids, there'll be plenty of balloons and hotdogs. The fun starts at noon. Folks, we sure hope you're enjoying the day as much as we are – we've got a barn burner here. It's two out in the ninth…"

When the lightning bolt struck, the power went out and so did Timmy's bland radio chatter. His sharp, pointy, electrified chin wiggled as his attention shifted to the present tense. "What the hell was that!?" he asked, like a nasally cat. Hippy Girl Receptionist fielded the question, "Holy shit! I have no idea." Sales Manager came in with a flashlight, "Did you see that?" He didn't wait for an answer, "A bolt of lightning just hit the company sign." I immediately appointed myself head of the "let's go home" committee, but confusion and empty speculation took the stage and I was pushed to the wing. "Where did it come from?" they wondered, "It's so sunny outside."

When Chief Moustache stepped out of his office the chaos was complete. He'd been cutoff in the middle of having phone sex with his mistress and was not happy about it. In fact, he was still at half mast and a little out of breath when he emerged from his office demanding satisfaction. No one was allowed to disappoint him. Sales Manager jumped in, "A bolt of lightning hit the company sign and knocked the power out, Chief." Chief Moustache's blood returned to his head, "Well let's go take a look, then. Everybody stay put." Off they went to inspect the damage at twice the rate of incompetence.

Timmy saw the lightning event as an ominous sign, thought perhaps he should mend his ways. On the other hand, I argued that God himself was helping us take the motherfuckers down.

A couple weeks later, Chief Moustache handed over all the company checkbooks to Sir Timmy Tatters. The lightning bolt had gotten Chief Moustache to thinking about the future. It was time to start spending more time with his mistress – shit like that.

I went to work on Timmy, "Look what that lightning bolt put in your lap, Timmy." He didn't need much of a push, still he was stressed. He sucked up half a joint, coughed up a lung and triggered his asthma, "I wonder how much I can take without anyone noticing?"

"You'll figure it out."

Because of the slash and burn nature of the business, Chief Moustache had several SPIFF Incorporateds going all at once: same invoice, different names and sets of moustaches. The SPIFFS were doing very well, easily around a $100,000 each in profit every month. Whatever it was, Timmy dutifully pulled out his calculator and stole to the penny.

I became the bulldog of accounts receivable. I started policing the moustaches, "This fucking order better be solid." When a moustache got a big sale I'd clap like a monkey – come on man I got bills to pay – whores to lay – rubics to cube. Know what I mean? My drug dealer is coming over, then Christmas, half my friends think I'm the drug dealer, the other half don't care as long as it keeps rolling in their favor and anyway who cares about this, or that, the world is god-awful, so what're ya gonna do?

All my shady friends shook me down for wads of cash, "Hey, Mick, ya wonderful son of a bitch, borrow me a thousand dollars. It's important. Pay you back, promise." I gave without remorse because that was how I took it. I was a wolf, my very own sinister creation. Compelled for some unknown reason to kick, punch and bite at whatever was there – tweaking my levers – no future – no way to communicate – no way to understand – the distance too great. There's no death stare between us. The eyes I look into say, "Come and kill me, I'm dead anyway."

Even the most malevolent wolf will only slash thirty or forty before becoming too depressed to continue. "Why do they all want to die so cruelly?" He'll say to himself as he heads for the hills.

He takes to the hills because he has seen the wrath of the owners. With black eyes they'll come – in a rage over any free-born son who refuses to comply with their property rights, "Who is this fucker to steal what is rightfully ours? He'll pay a thousand for one in bone, flesh, and blood with poisons and bullets and traps and iron bars and razor wire. There has to be a lesson taught, freedom requires it, people. This wolf will eat your children. Come now, gather together. We'll watch over you. Talk to the minister here, he'll give you the details."

Swedish Geisha

I met a girl, about my age, tall and slender, a virgin she said. I believed her. I had to work on her for almost a year. It was quaint how she would jerk me off then clean me up with a warm wet rag. She was my Swedish Geisha. She was saving herself for some unknown reason, when and where we did it was up to her. It had to be perfect, or at least well organized. That's the only way she would have it – full-on middle American – color coordinated, curling ironed, hair sprayed, blow dried, made up, panty hosed, fine knit sweatered, slacked, or blue jeaned.

I drove through the silos, the red river valley, the gray gray gray, with her sitting on the passenger side humming to herself, looking in her compact mirror, smoothing her skin, applying lipstick, clicking it shut, looking out the window, a long sigh, a change in position, another, adjusting the collar, scratching an itch, pulling down the visor and flipping open the mirror, moving in for a close-up, adding some mascara, flipping it shut, opening her purse, taking out a stick of gum, looking over, "Would you like some?"

"No, thanks."

One Friday night, Swedish Geisha dolled herself up and dragged me to a house party in Northeast Minneapolis. There was a giant gaggle of her acquaintances farting around a keg in the kitchen. Swedish Geisha paraded me around the house and I met all the substantial people in her life, the close confidantes, the sworn enemies, the gossip hounds, the drunken whores, the bullies, the brats, the beer chuggers, the ex-kissers and fondlers and borrowers and lenders. Swedish Geisha and I went drink for drink and beer for beer, then wandered off into the night and ended up rolling around on a lawn full of dog shit. We didn't notice at first. We staggered to my car and piled in and, as I was fumbling with the keys, Swedish Geisha noticed the smell. She flipped on the dome light and screamed. I was head to toe covered with dog shit. It was then that the smell hit me and I fell out of the car gagging and peeling off my clothes. I left it all in a heap, there on the side of the road. Swedish Geisha had just a smidge of dog shit on her ruffled blouse. She slipped out of it and stuck it in the trunk – she'd wash it out later. I took her back to my unfurnished apartment and she jerked my dick with a dry hand while I poked around her pussy with a couple fingers and begged for a couple strokes, "Just let me slide it in – I'll pull it right back out I promise."

"No!"

Ten months passed and Swedish Geisha was finally ready. I should have known, the place was immaculate, fine music, perfumed air. It wasn't even her place. She still lived with her parents. She was house-sitting for a friend. We fucked nice and easy in their bed and after that, we fucked every two hours for the next year and a half.

She was so sweet and conservative – an endless heart, a quick laugh, a thin scarf, frost bit ears from standing at the bus stop. She preferred the missionary position, but made up for it by having the sweetest pussy ever and endless legs. Her pussy could get a grip on my shaft like no other – so fucking perfect – it was like God himself was reaching down and working my member. Her pussy would just draw the sperm out of me. I knocked her up four fucking times, kept breaking the rubber, or too late pulling out. I tried to surrender, "Maybe we should get married," but she knew better. She saw how her pretty girlfriends and I were always together. She was too young. She wanted to hold out for a future something. Anyway, it would ruin her life. Besides, what was I but a broken down clerk in disguise – not even a good disguise if you cared to look – throwing money away just as fast as I stole it – a raging alcoholic prophet – metaphysically broke – the tip of my cock for unwed mothers – alms for the poor. I bought a pissy party house with Timmy, stuck a shiny speedboat in the garage, drove a ridiculous sports car into the ground.

Swedish Geisha and I took little trips together just like grown ups. We'd get on the road and drive and find a motel and I would run inside and sign us in as husband and wife. "You folks just passing through?"

"That's right, the wife and I are on our honeymoon."

"In South Dakota!? Well, we do have a room with a water bed."

"We'll take it."

As I was saying, she still lived with her parents. They were kindly folks, true and sincere, quite the opposite of me. They would saunter off to bed leaving Swedish Geisha and I watching TV. Not five minutes later, we'd be on the floor under a thin blanket. She was a nervous ninny, "Not yet, let's wait until we're sure they're asleep."

"I plan on doing it then, as well." I'd pull her summer shorts down and she'd slip a leg out, leaving them to dangle on the other, just in case she heard something, then she'd quickly slip her leg back in and pull them back in place, which she was always doing, right in the middle of a fuck, "What was that!?"

"What?"

"I thought I heard something."

"It was nothing."

Swedish Geisha was always a few weeks pregnant and walking through the protesters to the clinic door. I tagged along, it was the least I could do. The protesters met us in the parking lot. They pleaded for the egg, prayed for the soul. When that didn't work, they screamed, doomed us to hell. The closer we got to the door, the more desperate they became, "Don't do it!" "The baby inside you is a life." "You've got no right!" "You'll burn in hell, whore!" "Murderer! Murderer! Murderer!"

Swedish Geisha was a wreck before she got inside the clinic. The whole goddamn mess traumatized her. She went on the pill.

The Line

Timmy Tatters was on a campaign of self-improvement, superficial things mostly, the kind money could buy. He had some hair plugs installed to hide his receding hairline. They were sliced from the back of his neck and planted in perfect little rows in front. You could cut them with a combine. He decided that his new look required a new vehicle, so he bought himself a fully loaded four wheel drive pickup truck. He said, "I paid cash for it, let's take it for a spin." It was a Friday, late afternoon. We collected my old pal Country, who was now living in St. Paul, and he suggested a drive to River Falls. His girlfriend was going to school there. She lived in a dorm on campus with her best friend from high school. They snuck us down a cinderblock hall to their metal door and cinderblock room.

We started the night off by doing "the Line" at some backwater tavern – Country's girlfriend tagged along. If you could drink "the Line" (21 different imported beers) in less than two hours, they gave you a t-shirt that proudly displayed that fact, then pointed you toward the parking lot.

Timmy was fresh off a DWI and didn't want to risk another, so he threw me the keys and pretended he was doing me a favor, "Hey, Mick, take the keys, I know you're just dying to give my new truck a try." We stuffed ourselves into the truck and made our way back into town and another bar. I met an enthusiastic girl and hammered down a couple long island ice teas with her. She grabbed my hand and led me to the dance floor. I was too fucked up for that. I scared her off with my drunken advances. Really, I just needed a shoulder to lean on, but all her enthusiasm was gone. She said she had to take a piss, so left me to stand on my own. The place was kind of blurry, the lights were certainly dim. I couldn't find any of my losers. I thought I saw Timmy, in his brown knit sweater with a clown on the front – they were practically twins, they were scowling at something in the corner. Timmy had his thumbs hooked in his watch pockets and he was swaying like a stem of barley.

I spotted Long Island Ice Tea back from the pisser and thought I'd try another dance. I staggered over on an S curve, knocked drinks out of hands, was pushed from behind by wet t-shirts and pants, stumbled forward knocking into more drinks – it was a chain reaction. Long Island Ice Tea kept backing away, she was no longer receiving, "Get away from me! God! You're such a fucking slob." I wobbled in front of her and let go that wonderful fucked up laugh of the demon who is forced to wear the human clothes and play the human endeavor. If she only knew. I was a fucking slob all right – that was just the beginning. I added stupid braggart, "You don't know what you're missing." I pulled out a twenty, tore it in half and threw it at her, "Here's a little something you can remember me by when I'm a rich and famous artist." She quickly gathered up both halves and laughed, "What a fucking idiot." She looked around the circle of curious drinkers, "Did you see that? he just gave me twenty dollars." She laughed again, said, "Thanks," and left.

I stumbled into Country and his girlfriend at the brass rail. We knocked down a couple of shots of tequila and poured ourselves into everyone's way, according to them we were leaving a stain. Then Timmy appeared before us as a poorly executed paint-by-numbers. He wanted to leave. "Stop being a pussy and drink this shot of Tequila." He didn't have a choice in the matter.

Before we knew it, the night was over. They kicked everyone out and, though I was clearly the least able, we got into Timmy's brand new pickup and I drove. Right down the middle of the ice covered road I hit the gas hard, the tires slipped, the speedometer zipped between thirty-five and one hundred ten. I screamed out the window with all my might, "Whaaa-hooo! I love this fucking world and everyone in it!" I was at my peak, I could reach up into the sky. Meanwhile, Country's girlfriend, almost sober and well below the clouds, filed several complaints. She was also the navigator, "Take a right here!" I was still howling out the window, invincible in the cold, dark night. I cranked the wheel hard to the right without even looking. The moon was in the east, climbing. We made the corner, but the backend kept coming around. I waved hello and cranked it hard the other way and waved hello to that side as well. I repeated that pattern until we bumped over a curb and slammed into a tree. The tree caught the front left quarter panel and crumpled it into the hood.

Timmy hit the roof, then, hit it again. We fell out of the cab and inspected the damage. It was pretty bad. I didn't care. I started in on Timmy, "Dude, it's fine you can hardly see it. Slap a little Bondo on it and it'll be good as new."

Timmy stood there with his thumbs hooked shaking his head, "Dude, you wrecked my truck."

"Come on, Timmy, it's barely a scratch, rub a little turtle wax on there and buff it out." The more I flipped him over, the more he shook his head, the sad clown, but that just drove me further. Country jumped in with a Spicoli, "Dude, I can fix it. My dad's got, like, this ultimate set of tools. I can fix it."

Timmy drove the rest of the way back to the dorm. I gave them the bleary eye while they pulled me down the cinderblock hall. I was to sleep in the best friend's bed, the top bunk – she was still out on the town. Country gave me a drunken boost and I laid where I landed and managed to get the room to stop spinning. Oh, the happy misery of life – this emptiness inside – it never gets better.

The first time I had too much to drink was when the Old Man dragged us to a tractor pull – super charged tractors pulling heavy loads down a dirt path in corn country – in front of a bleachered crowd of a couple thousand. We arrived in the Old Man's Ford Supercab pickup truck. It wasn't that super. We were joined by our neighbors, the Junkyard family. They came in a school bus the junkyard king had converted for just such occasions. He'd built in some bunk beds, added a stove, sink, cabinets and a refrigerator full of beer and Shasta. He also left some of the original bench seats near the front.

Our armies met at the gate and we were ordered to stay close. Once we hit the main drag though, Junkyard Kid and I cut out and went back to the bus. We sipped Shasta's, sat on the bench seats, tuned the radio and dared each other to chug a beer. We were thirteen. There were other teens in the parking lot. They ambled over to see what had been done to their school bus. We let them onboard. They liked the changes. The subject of beer came up again. There was a fifteen-year-old up to the challenge. We watched him guzzle one down. That got the ball rolling. We spilled beer, played bloody knuckles, cranked the stereo, forgot ourselves, trashed the bus. Junkyard King and the Old Man appeared out of nowhere and scattered our crowd of teen drunks. I got up to leave myself, but was pushed back against the refrigerator and given a plastic bag while Junkyard Kid got the mop. We were put to the task while Junkyard King and the Old Man took our seats and finished our beers...

I was just about to drop off, safe for the night, when Best Friend climbed onto the bunk and demanded I roll to the side. The room began to spin again. I puked over the edge of the bunk on all the sleeping bags below. There was a mad scramble. They pulled me off the bunk. I stumbled into the closet and puked all over the shoes.

They grabbed me again and pushed me out the door. I puked in the cinderblock hall. I puked wherever they put me.

The next morning we all had tremendous hangovers, but Timmy was most miserable of all. His colors had run. He looked like his truck. I couldn't stop snickering. I was coming unglued. It seemed hilarious to me that Timmy was so upset over a truck he didn't even pay for. It flipped me out for some reason so I gave him the big speech, "Fucking A, Timmy, rubber stamp yourself another roll, what's a couple grand among thieves? If you're gonna steal, steal big – the Robber Barons knew that way back when. Don't start thinking you're a pillar in the community like our dear inflated President. You pay the PR people for that – destroy – destroy – destroy – do it bigger and better – let the lawyers dicker the numbers – they don't make bombs for storing – you gotta keep things moving – and praise the glory – be humble in public – give them a slogan – something soluble in water – and throw some parades – don't forget to posture – repeat the word "freedom" – tie it to fear – and merchandise – pretend that the system is naturally occurring – back it up by smashing anyone who disagrees – hire just enough of the disenfranchised and put them to work patrolling the rest. Now, take a couple aspirin and stop crying over a stupid fucking truck."

Lam Chops

I was empty deep down, bored, depressed, tired of everything, mostly myself. What does this life mean? Other than these sad facts and remedies and garbage cans and I'll poke you and you poke me and we'll slow poke down the line.

I quit SPIFF Incorporated. Suddenly, I was done taking for a living. I still held fast to my notion that the game was rigged and the world was a farce, but from then on I wouldn't steal a thing – not with sleight of hand shenanigans, rubber contracts, price fixing, profit taking, etc. I didn't have it in me anymore, I wanted to forget that the whole SPIFF Incorporated thing ever happened. But that's not how the universe works.

The phone rang. It was one of the moustaches from SPIFF Incorporated, "Hey, Mick, ya stupid son of a bitch, Chief Moustache found some checks with your name on them."

"I don't know what you're talking about."

"Whatever. From what I hear there's already a detective on the case, just thought I'd give you a heads up."

I put down the phone and thought, well, this is it then, the end of everything just like I wished for. I hung my head and stared at the floor. There was a little tear in the gray carpet, I did it myself several months before with a steak knife, stinking drunk. The carpet was thin, the particle board was thinner, I drove it right through the basement ceiling. And here I thought I would wither into the night of the rest of my life.

When Timmy got word the law was coming for us, he freaked, "I've got to get out of here, man, NOW! I'll empty my bank accounts and change my identity and live on the lam until this thing blows over. What's the statute of limitations on this sort of thing – seven years?"

"I don't fucking know."

"Mick, grab all your money and let's go."

"Dude, I'm broke, it'll be up to you to pay."

It was true. I had maybe a couple hundred dollars to my name. I had blown everything, it didn't seem right to save it. I fancied myself a Viking come down from up North to rob the village, the castle, the monastery. Rape and pillage was the game, I was willing to admit it. I wasn't interested in long-term relationships, especially not with that goddamn money, it was stolen to be spent, not stuffed into savings.

Suddenly I felt great, an immediate goal was all I needed – back to Mexico. I knew what to do with those lovely senoritas this time around. I threw my crap in a plastic garbage bag (just like old times), stuck it behind the driver's seat and locked up the pissy party house. Timmy jam-packed his leather luggage and followed in his car. We headed for Chicago, drove all night and pulled in early the next morning. We set ourselves up in a motel in Skokie and dropped into the city for some sight-seeing. We went to the top of the Sears Tower. It was funny as hell to be standing with all the tourists, fugitives of the law. We blended right in, "Wow, look at that." "Oh my, we're really up in the air." "Get a picture of that." "Is that Wrigley field?"

We hung out in Chicago until paranoia set in and everyone looked to be spying on us. We hit the road again, heading west out of Illinois, across Iowa into Nebraska with its blankets of straw covering the sandy ditch and old tires circling the bottom of every fence post and telephone pole to keep the sand from blowing away. Somewhere in the middle, a highway patrol passed slowly in the left lane. After he cleared my front bumper, he slowed down and then I was gaining on him. I took my foot off the gas so I wouldn't. My heart was snapping in my chest like the rat-tat-tat-tat of Speed Freak's rubber band knuckles. Mr. Highway Patrol slowed even more; so did I. We crawled along the freeway fading into the teens. I thought, what in the hell am I doing? Instead of outrunning the highway patrol, I'm out-slowing him? What could this possibly achieve? Nothing. Mr. Highway Patrol hit his brakes, wheeled around behind and flipped on the siren and lights. I pulled to the side of the road, a dead duck. Mr. Highway Patrol walked up to my window and asked, "What the hell were you doing back there?"

"Ah, what do you mean?"

"Why did you slow down like that?"

I made something up, "Ah, because you slowed down and I didn't want to pass you on the right and I thought maybe there was something going on up ahead that I didn't know about so I was following your lead." I'm good with off-the-cuff bullshit.

Mr. Highway Patrol swallowed it and went on, "I pulled you over because you don't have a front license plate and I believe that in the state of Minnesota you are required to have a front plate." He was good with off-the-cuff bullshit as well, "I'll need to see your driver's license please."

I handed it over and while he checked me out on the computer, I sat in my car with a punched out gut, waiting for the rest of the local law enforcement to descend upon me and carry me away to the nearest jail cell. How many jail cells were between here and

Minnesota? How many cuffs? Lines to stand behind? It seemed immeasurable, these were my thoughts. But then Mr. Highway Patrol was back at my window and I signed for the greatest most magnificent traffic ticket in the history of the world. I drove through the white sands with a song in my heart and a tidal wave blew over me and I rode it on down the highway.

A few miles ahead I found Timmy hiding in his car on the far side of an overpass. He'd seen it go down from his rearview mirror and thought he was next. "Mick! What happened? I thought you were done for."

"Listen, Timmy, it's obvious the law isn't even looking for us."

"Yeah, we'll have to check with some people back home and see what's going on."

"While we're out here, let's see the Southwest."

We hit Colorado and drifted into Denver the day after an early spring snowstorm. The snow was piled high and already melting, the streets were wet with the runoff. The great Rocky Mountains leaned in from the west while we ate at a fast-food joint. It didn't seem right to see that, but come to this.

We turned south and drove all the way to Las Cruces, New Mexico, in one sitting. We set ourselves up in a thin motel and made some tentative calls back home. There was nothing going on, but there would be. It was on the breeze, the scent of some ominous thing. We'd need to get across the border soon, but Timmy had the jitters, "I don't know about this, Mick, what the hell will I do in Mexico?"

I gave him a Hollywood line, "Dude, this is between having to run forever and not running at all."

"Jesus Christ, Mick, can't you take anything seriously?" I really couldn't.

Las Cruces was windswept and hot. We kept the air-conditioning on high and our voices on low. Timmy said, "I'm just so damn stressed."

"Hey, Timmy, let's hit the bar for a few drinks and unwind a little."

"Oh alright, but I'm not letting you drive."

I was in a hell of a mood after a dozen beers and fourteen shots of tequila. Timmy advised, "Better cool it, Mick, people are staring."

"No thanks, Timmy, I haven't hit bottom." I stumbled around the place bumping into the boys at the bar and yelling, "Words don't mean shit, man, words don't mean shit!" I found the front door and stepped out into a blinding light. I cupped my eyes and staggered up to a Harley rider, who was trying in vain to kick-start his Harley by the side of the road. I yelled at him, "Stay off the fucking freeway punk! Hee hee hee ha ha ha... or I'll run you over with my hunk of skylab." Harley Rider was not amused. He jumped off his bike and came around front, "You talking shit to me man?"

It turned out that the boys at the bar were all Harley riders. They formed a ring and soon enough I was knocked to a sidewalk made of raspy concrete with a layer of biting dust blown in from parts unknown. Two Harleys dragged me along, while three or four others followed along kicking at me. Someone leaned over and cracked my nose and lip. Thankfully, I was properly anesthetized and hardly felt a thing, but I did make a few mental notes along the way – ah, the angry mules are at it again – certainly this was a long time coming – this must be what the bottom feels like – horrible – but then you get used to it, like a bone in the throat – come on fuckers is that all you got? I deserve worse and now you're walking away? I spotted a bloody cocksucker in a window, the same long diagonal crack – me, at the end of the road.

I propped myself against an adobe wall. The blazing wind, that blew constant and dirty down the road, felt ice-cold. I shivered like I was still under the last breathing tree. Maybe I was. This bottom didn't feel so bad, what was I afraid of before? I couldn't remember. Timmy walked up and I asked, "Where'd everybody go?"

"I bought them a round. I told you that was gonna happen, man. You're one messed up motherfucker." Drenched in the cold breeze, I never felt better.

I wiped some blood from my face and rubbed it between my thumb and forefinger. I was surprised how slippery it was and how quickly it dried. I rolled it into a ball and pressed it to the wall behind me – finally – some time to contemplate. How long will that ball of blood be there? Will it wash away with the next rainfall? Christ, it's dry here, does it ever rain at all? I'll come back tomorrow and check up on it, but then, why would I do that? One blood stain is the same as the next, I suppose. I took the deepest breath ever and choked on it. What the hell does Las Cruces mean anyhow? I said to Timmy, "Time to go home and face this thing."

Old Testament God

Word got out while I was on the lam. All my friends and acquaintances ransacked the pissy party house. Used the key under the brick, everybody knew about it. They took everything, including the stove, refrigerator and shiny boat. What was stolen, was stolen again – it was perfect. I slept on the puke-stained carpet in my room with my head propped on a folded pair of acid washed jeans – stripped away. I finger scratched the carpet fibers, toe tickled the gray gray gray, waited for the clock to start ticking again. No future to spruce up for, just the impending doom of the legal system crushing out all other thoughts in my head. I quit-claimed the pissy party house to Timmy, he still thought he had a future.

I sold the ridiculous sports car and shelled out for a high rent lawyer suggested by a relative. The lawyer wore a cowboy hat and boots, just like the Old Man. My lawyer was a cowboy. He seemed to know what he was doing. He confirmed that charges were pending, gave it to me straight, "You'll probably get eighteen months in the state pen. In the meantime, get a job, it'll look good."

I made the rounds like before, but it wasn't the same. All my ransacking friends gathered together in groups opposite my vertical position and shared snickers and squinted gestures and tipsy rumors and quick underhanded glances in my direction. They didn't bother getting the story from me. Their version was better anyway. Country kept me up to date on the latest narrative, "Hey, Mick, the word on the street is you stole over two million dollars and you were running a coke ring and involved in cock fighting and hamster rape."

"No shit? Well then it must be true."

"Yeah, that's what I said."

Cowboy rang me up one day. It was time to turn myself over to the legal system. I went early one morning to the Hennepin County Detention Center. They let me right in, gave me a frisking, a finger printing, camera shots, measured my cranium, "Yep, this one's a keeper."

I was led to a holding cell for twenty, I counted fifty-seven. It was a milling crowd. An inmate approached me, he looked like a regular, "What're ya in for?"

"I don't know I wasn't paying attention."

"Got any smokes?"

"No."

"Then what are you good for?"

"I don't know."

A few hours later I was chained to four other inmates, one of them was a dude on crutches, the other three were already wearing county colors. A couple of armed guards led us down a hallway to a freight elevator, then down another hallway and another and another – lefts, rights, ups, downs, the gray gray gray of high civilization – ending in a small gray room. We kept our eyes straight ahead, staring at nothing, barely breathing.

They unhooked the inmate whose number was up. They crosschecked it on a clipboard; it was just a fucking job. They kept the rest of us standing there chained together while the single-cuffed took his turn somewhere. Then it was my turn. I was unhooked and pushed through the same door into a courtroom full of people. Cowboy was there. He motioned. I stood next to him and tried to look pathetic. It wasn't difficult. They kept tight to the schedule, laid out the preliminaries and gathered in the necessities, "Shall he be released on his own recognizance?"

"He did surrender willingly, your Honor."

"Does he have a prior record?"

"No, your Honor."

Somewhere in the middle I got lost but they didn't, "How does the defendant plead?"

There I was staring into the distance like I was still a kid at the edge of the woods standing on a dirt pile...

The Old Man shoveled a wagon load of it each spring and sprinkled it on the sandy garden. I loved playing on it. In fact, I considered it mine. I created advanced civilizations on the shoveled away slope, my little army men played the civilians.

I got a plastic pail, filled it with water, lugged it to the top and set it in place above the city. I dug a nail out of my pocket and punched a hole near the bottom. The nail was a built in stopper when it was pushed all the way to the flat head. I pulled it out and pointed the hole toward my city. A wonderful river was born. It wagged its way down a hand scooped ditch, right through my magnificent city. I used another bucket to keep my river flowing full time and the army men and I relaxed and dreamt of gold or whatever.

Ah, but I was an Old Testament God. I was moody. I plagued my city and army men. I stomped the shit out of my creations with a sudden fury, didn't know what I was doing until I was doing it. By then it was too late – a tornado doesn't change its mind, it lives until it dies. I wedged firecrackers into the army men and blew them sky high. I tipped the pail over and swelled my little river a thousand times. I did the same with the second bucket, five or ten seconds of raging river and my city was wiped out. I lorded over them, "This will be a lesson for you to never defy me."

"But what did we do to deserve this and how can we avoid this in the future?"

"I don't know. Make something up."…

The court repeated the question, "How does the defendant plead?" Cowboy gave them my line, "Not guilty, your Honor." I nodded my head in agreement.

They set a court date, then, pushed me back through the door and I was re-cuffed to the chain, where I resumed my straight ahead stare.

We were stuffed together in another cell further down the line. We scattered to the benches – just us in a decent size cell – a place to relax. We had gone through something together. What could we do, but laugh and tell stories? "I was just walking down the street at four in the morning, minding my own fuckin' business, when the cops come up on me yellin', 'What're you doing carrying that TV down the street in the middle of the night?' I said to them, 'It's none of your damn business what I do with my TV.' Shit! Goddamn! A black man can't walk down the sidewalk with a TV in his hands? You know what I'm sayin'? Then they wanted to see the receipt. I didn't have the damn receipt!" He yelled at the cell door, "Let me out I'm innocent!" Then he laughed and laughed and nearly fell over. The dude on crutches jumped in with a few of his twisted little stories of serious alcohol and cocaine poisoning. He lost his job – his house – his wife – even still, he didn't seem in a bad way about it. You could say that he was almost jolly. His eyes would shine out when he told one of his crazy coke stories or some flipped-over-car-in-the-ditch alcoholic binge.

After a few hours together we were split up and I was led away to a tiny cell, one cot all to myself. They fed me beef hash, carrot sticks and milk. They slid it through the steel door on a tin tray just like in the movies. I giggled like an idiot at the thought of it. It felt good. I shivered under a cardboard blanket and thought, this is still better than baling hay with the Old Man...

Every summer the Old Man piled work on us with gusto. We kissed away the carnival, the Fourth of July was for baling hay. On top of the world he was, dragging us around a bumpy field. We were attached by wagon and hay baler to the Old Man and his beloved Allis Chalmers. They whistled the same tune, over and over, flat notes mostly.

Big sister and I suffering – united in our contempt for the singer – the laugher – the delighter of our misery. Sweating, weak kneed, me with hay fever, sneezing, wheezing, itchy, homicidal feeling, dreaming – the carnival was sure to be the most magnificent thing, especially this year.

The nicotine carnies and their broken dreams dressed up in scabs, cigarette butts, rumbling town to town with plenty of time to think about things they'll do nothing about. Working the same dirt lot that, come winter, would be our ice rink with a little wood fired warming house – a long, narrow plywood box – a ramp in from the street, a ramp out to the ice, a retiree sitting inside watching our every move, cutting us off before we could, take a breath, form a sentence.

Our skates didn't fit. They were bought on sale the previous summer. They always underestimated our ability to grow. They wrote our names on them like it made a difference. Our pinched toes, no room for an extra sock, we froze from the bottom up. We spent most of the time in the warming house, taking our skates off and putting them on, taking them off and putting them on. It was confusing. By the end of the day I was wearing a Tommy K. and a Mark S. The retiree would complain about the noise, always about the noise. He was a real old time crank, sitting next to a red hot cast iron caboose stove and sputtering obscenities whenever we let the cold air in. It was at least 110 degrees in the far corner where my friends and I bloodied our chapped knuckles, wagged our tongues at each other, who would get the last laugh, the final insult, before the retiree cussed us out the door? Two more laps around and we were back for a greeting...

The end was near. The wagon was stacked ten bales high and squared off. We rose with our last hope of making the carnival night life, then out of the thin blue Junkyard King arrived with a second wagon that sent the Old Man into another realm of glory. This was his day just like all the others. Everyone took a back seat including the Mom. He kept us all together in the rearview mirror, goading us, demon bubbling, gurgling, waxing bullshit, wisecracking. Our suffering induced howling laughter from him, clear from the gut, great spasms of joy. He took another nasty turn, "You ain't got it so bad. Take another salt pill and stop the goddamn pouting."...

The jail door opened and the guard placed his orders, "Come with me, here's your crap, sign here, you're free to leave. But don't leave the state. We'll be seeing you again. This thing is habitual, that's scientifically proven. We won't be surprised if we see you next week for something else."

Anglo on a Jet Ski

After all the taking and throwing away I was back where I started – just me and a big old double-hulled rusty tanker that needed a muffler. I bought it for three hundred dollars and I drove it into a depression – it slipped into neutral.

I had the same crazy dream every night. I was in the belly of a whale – I was a clerk in charge of the record keeping – the whale contained millions of years worth of data – the paper was made of dried plankton – the entries were written in crayon. There was no let-up on the in-flow, it was just one long horrible story. I couldn't keep up with the data entry – crayons kept snapping in two – the whale lost its sense of direction – started thrashing about – somehow I hung on – who did this before me, I wondered? – it seemed like it had always been me – one way or another – it was worse than the turkey plant but I kept going – worked harder than I ever had before.

The plankton paper could not be filed away until it had been properly colored in – it piled up, up, up – I fell further and further behind – the whale suffocated and died – I rode the carcass forever – I crayoned a "help wanted" sign on its back – peered down the blow hole – was picked up by an Anglo on a jet ski – Anglo delivered me to the edge of the world and threw me over.

I awoke with the stench of dead whale, flakes of plankton paper under my nails and jars of blubber in the refrigerator. The stink saturated the butter. I was stuck in that nightmare all spring and summer. Then, quite suddenly, my double-hulled tanker popped into gear and I drove out of there. People noticed. They were even wide-eyed about it, "Hey, you're moving around again."

"I am?" I looked in the rearview mirror. It was true. The background was once again receding.

Ogled

My moods were all over the place. I went from pious reformer to lascivious defendant to down-and-out drunkard all in a weekend. I took some classes at the University – I had a long list of things to get to. I rented a room in a condemned house in the Dinkytown neighborhood. My roommates were mainly students, and like me on the, I'll-go-when-I-can plan. There were four of us – five, when my old pal Country moved in after getting the boot from his girlfriend.

One of the roommates was a rail-thin acne-layered guy from New Jersey. He didn't let his defects get him down. "My old man has loads of money, but he's one hard ass son of a bitch. I'm the best thing to hit this town. I'm gonna row a scull down the Mississippi river for charity."

Another roommate was a fat ruddy fella who went about five-five around the belly and up from the ground. He was obsessed with getting laid. He was still a virgin and desperate to end that part of his life. He drank beer by the gallon and dreamt of one day having a beer tap on his refrigerator door.

The last roommate was a squat bull elephant – a hard partier and way too rowdy. He was the first guy to break something or quarrel with the cops, "I only fuck fat chicks, man. You don't know what you're missing – getting lost in the folds – and they try harder – skinny chicks just lay there."

We kept the parties going every Thursday through Sunday – the kind you would imagine in a condemned house. It was practically a riot – only a matter of physics as to when we'd fall through the floor. We practiced interior nonconformity – people wrote on the walls – it had a tribal flavor – the cops put us on a list – it was usually lit up like Christmas.

I blew most of my student loan money on an electric guitar and amp instead of paying tuition. I left school with the same long list of things to get to.

Country had a job working as a carpenter's apprentice. They paid him a lower wage and made him take classes to prove he was serious. "Hey, Mick, they're looking for a labor dude down at the construction site – nine bucks an hour is what it pays."

"I can do that – put in a good word for me."

"I'll have to make something up."

"No doubt about it."

I went down to the construction site to meet the foreman and to show him I was enthused about the job, I laughed at his stupid jokes and helped him ogle his new stripper calendar. He tacked it to the wood paneling next to last year's edition, then he hollered, "You're fucking hired. Be here tomorrow morning by six a.m. sharp so you can fill out some paperwork."

I thought to myself, tomorrow, isn't that Friday? I'd like a little notice before you hire me, at least a week. If not, then how about the weekend? We were gonna tie one on tonight. I made plans this morning with my condemned roommates. I wrote it on the back of my hand, 'Get Hammered' in black ink.

The plan went off without a hitch. By nine o'clock I was pitching an alcoholic fit, just like the others, sitting in a sports bar yelling over a half dozen pitchers of beer and a basket of chicken wings, "Mine's longer!" "No, mine's longer." Somebody suggested, "Hey, let's get a keg and look for disaster." Everyone agreed. Country and I picked up the keg and some tequila while the condemned roommates canvassed the bars and brought a condemned crowd to our condemned house.

I was holding court by myself, next to a window, when Ruddy made his way over and said he had a gram of coke and was throwing a little party in the basement, "Dude, if you can get some girls down there you can have some too. But let's be discreet about this I don't want a crowd."

"Hey, Ruddy, I'll need an advance." That perked me up some. "All right, Ruddy, I'll be your personal pimp and don't worry, I'll be discreet about it. But the first one I tell will be like telling all the others. Let's just hope they're mostly potheads."

I scanned the room and spotted a triangle of women. I floated over on a coked breeze, "Do you ladies go to school here?" Nope, two angles worked on an assembly line in Anoka and the third angle was a hairdresser. I got to the point, "Say, we're having a little party downstairs. It has its own special ingredient – sniff sniff – would you like to come?" Well, of course they did. I pointed them toward the basement door and followed behind. On the way down the stairs I fell in love with Hairdresser, such a cute little apple ass wrapped in tight white corduroy pants. I can't remember her face. We hit the bottom step and Ruddy peeked around a makeshift curtain that was dividing the room. Satisfied, he pulled it back, "Hello, ladies, please enter." We bowed our heads in prayer, one at a time. The door above opened wide, "Hey, anybody down there?" We didn't answer. We stood together behind the curtain like snowmen. They came down anyway.

Three more squeezed behind the curtain. It was getting tight in there. One of the Assembly Lines reached out and pinched my ass. I made a big deal of it. I jumped in the air, the Assembly Lines giggled. I looked at Hairdresser and pretended it was her. She threw such a frown in my direction and said, "No fucking way!" I didn't get it. She turned her back and I squeezed in tight behind while the Assembly Lines bumped up against me.

Hairdresser wasn't interested, not even the least bit interested. I only knew that I had to have her. She split out the back of the curtain and headed upstairs all by herself. "Hey, Hairdresser, where are you running off to?" Without turning around she said, "Away from you."

I laughed it up, poured down more liquor, did a couple more lines of coke, then went upstairs to find her. I was hampered in my efforts by the Assembly Lines. As I was stalking Hairdresser, they were stalking me. They were tag teaming, I think. I couldn't tell them apart to tell. I backed one of them into a corner. She thought I was going to kiss her. She closed her eyes and tried to pull me close. I had to be honest, "Listen, goddamn it! I'm not interested, all right? All I'd do is fuck you and never call you again." "I love it when you talk dirty to me."

I spotted Hairdresser and gave it another whirl and another and another, until even Ruddy was ill, "Dude, leave her alone."

"Not until I pass out – I'm not a fucking quitter – this is America goddamn it, if there's a way there's a will."

Ruddy wasn't satisfied, so he poured me a shot of something and offered a toast, "Here's to ya passing out."

That was the one that did me in. I fell into the arms of an Assembly Line and she tucked me in bed. We spoon fucked for a bit. The alarm went off.

The Labor Pool

I arrived at the jobsite by six in the morning, as requested, but Foreman didn't show up until seven, just like everybody else. I shivered by the construction trailer in the below-freezing dark. It reminded me of my nights spent leaning against fish houses. I wanted to go back to that, before this fucking crime spree. I leaned against the trailer so low down and thought about my early years living in the mini-ranch house – a tiny two bedroom, built by a part-time carpenter who stood less than four-six. The ceiling pushed down on you and if you were anything over five-four, you had to duck the doorways. In the beginning, I didn't have a bedroom. I slept in the alcove just off the kitchen. No door, just a single bed and dresser pushed up against the back of the refrigerator. At night, when the goblins were asleep, I would climb on top of the dresser, reach for the cookie jar on top of the fridge, pluck out a few chocolate chip cookies and then, do it again and again, compulsively. I'd prop the remaining few into teepee structures and crawl back under the sheet.

Soon enough I had toothaches that rivaled my earaches. They pounded my head in tandem. I kept on eating though, stuck tissue in my ears to stop the bleeding, stared at the big black sky through paper curtains. The dull buzz of the refrigerator eventually put me to sleep in mid crumble. I dreamt of piss-fed alligators under my bed. I'd wake up at 3:00 a.m. with an arm over the side – dangling deliciously. Just before the gator snapped, I'd yank my arm out of the way and the bed would jump; all four posts would clear the floor. I knew I was blessed for something.

The Old Man was just starting to drag us back in time to the 1870's. He was dead set on turning his twenty acres of northern Minnesota into an old West horse ranch. He rebuilt the barn – made it bigger and bigger. Inside the barn he organized a tack room and filled it with saddles and bridles and curry combs and quirks (made with stiff braided leather). He included a workbench with a vise, a grinder, an assortment of hammers and saws, a little row of glass jars with nails, screws, nuts, bolts, pennies, bullets, and in the corner, a couple garbage cans full of horse feed. He directed the construction of a tamarack pole corral and fenced in a portion of his twenty acres. Weeknights and weekends were devoted to this task. We did it all ourselves, rolled out the wire and tacked it to a line of posts. He was serious about his fucking fence, it had to be straight as an arrow and twice as tight.

He believed that every good cowboy rode a Quarter horse, so he organized a family vacation out west to Montana, where he could scope out the right pregnant mare to start his new horsey brood. He found her in Ekalaka. I ate my first ranch breakfast in the only cafe in town: pancakes as big as the plate, hash browns, two eggs (over easy), bacon, toast, jelly, glass of milk, a shot of coffee. The high school had dinosaur bones on display. The people were mid-continental salty dogs, cowboy pirates on an eastern Montana plain. They were brimming – they believed in their big sky country – everything fit in perfectly. They had a high school rodeo for Christ's sake! We stood among them slightly hunched over. Life up North takes its toll.

We brought home a buckskin mare. Her name was Bear – and she was – a momma bear. She led with her teeth. When she laid back her ears you knew she was coming, snapping at whatever you had sticking out. I cleaned up after her and all her children (accumulating one at a time every couple years). In the winter time their collective shit mixed with regular intervals of snowfall and every day they went about packing it down in the corral. My general laziness meant I welcomed the snow. What was covered up remained so. Over time there was a glaciering effect. Springtime found me with a pick axe, striking through eighteen inches of manure and ice, piling one wheelbarrow load after another onto a great horseshit mountain at the edge of the woods. Pushing it along warped two-by-six boards through steaming foothills, the mountain growing sideways. The chipmunks couldn't care less. The worms were in heaven. The silent awe of the stick trees in waiting pose – same old early spring. Sometimes a jumbo jet passed overhead and it felt like a hangnail. All that white paint and only one straight line, emitting and spreading like my manure pile across the sky. And me in my muffled-down down-ness, fake fur parka, zip-up galoshes, icicle nose, frost bit, horse bit, life bit...

Foreman strolled up and slapped me on the back, "Sorry I'm late, I really tied one on last night." He handed me a tax form. "Fill this out and grab a hard hat. Oh, and if you see a HUD inspector make yourself scarce. You're not supposed to be here."

I was the construction site's one man clean up crew. I pumped the ditch, scraped the foundation, scrapped the lumber, unloaded the windows, swept the units. Whenever I fell behind, Foreman would grudgingly donate his weakest link to help me out for a few days. Weakest Link was well muscled in bib overalls, yet he was bushed less than twenty minutes into any operation. He was wonderful, "Man, I'm fading fast here, it's time for some empty calories." We'd bounce off the site in his rusty Cutlass and idle our way to the nearest convenience store where Weakest Link would fill a bag with donuts and prepackaged pastries, "Mmm, Bear Claws."

Back at the job site, we'd kick back in one of the mostly finished buildings and Weakest Link would have some very interesting things to say about working on a HUD funded construction project. "Everyone who works on a HUD funded project must be in a union or paid a union scale. What are they paying you?"

"Nine bucks an hour."

"Well, the union scale is at least fifteen."

"No shit? No wonder they want me to scram whenever an inspector comes by the site. Everybody's stealing from everybody. I'm gonna have to look into this."

"Hey man, you didn't hear it from me."

The townhouses were built in phases; three 16 unit buildings formed what they called a pod. About half way through the completion of a pod we'd break ground on another and so on and so forth.

The general contractor leased out the apartments well in advance of the building's completion. It was a disaster. It turned cold and nasty and production slowed to a crawl. Whenever the weather broke we'd play catch up, which led to mistakes, which caused more delays. The broken families who'd leased the townhouses would wander around looking at the bare ground where they were supposed to be living. I'd happen by and they would try to confirm with me what the general contractor had told them – that they'd be living there by the end of the month. I loved giving them the bad news, "Listen, you'll be lucky if you're living here in six months. But, hey, you didn't hear it from me."

When a hole was dug for a foundation, a cloud burst would fill it and then I'd have to crawl down and pump out the water. Hell isn't fire. Hell is mud. It was torture lugging the stiff fucking hoses and pump motor around, with mud everywhere and at varying depths, so I was never sure what I was stepping into. Then, having to start that impossible piece-of-shit pump motor. The whole operation had me screaming mad, "This goddamn son of a bitchin' goddamn motherfuckin' piece of goddamn fucking shit!"

I'd sit down in the mud and my ears would ache, like when I was a kid and my damaged ears could not tolerate the subzero weather between December and March...

I stayed off the ice. I quarantined myself inside my room. I refused to go to school on the basis that it was killing me. Those were the days when best friends boxed each other's ears in a fatalistic courtship of losing propositions. The pain was unbearable. I had a lot of best friends who wished to participate in mutual destruction, Franklin Elementary was like that. I wiped ear pus on every surface in every room, coated the bottom side of my desk with it, brushed it off on the hallway walls, in the cafeteria, on the wrestling mat.

Eventually my ear pus and I were forced back to school. I kept my head down. Once a day I squinted at the chalkboard. There was never anything interesting up there, anyway. I sat, day after day, like I was at the edge of one of the local iron ore pits – an-eight-hundred-foot deep toxic puddle pretending to be a lake. I'd put my toes in the water but I wouldn't jump in. No way was I gonna dive into that mess. I was a mountain man. Escape was the only thing on my mind – mission number one – a mandate – a grizzly bear – a true best friend.

I wanted away from the horrible menace of the local population. There were adults everywhere. I avoided the light of their eyes like the plague. I practiced the art of dysfunction. It worked. I was a total failure according to more than a few. No one knew I couldn't hear them. I got tired of saying, "What?" It annoyed them. I pretended I didn't understand. Most adults formed immediate conclusions. They pinned me down with their understanding.

I soon discovered that I was losing my eyesight as well. I could no longer see them yelling at me. What a relief! Every last one of them had something and the go ahead to use it. A day seldom passed when you didn't get hit by one of them. It was routine. Like three meals a day – starch and protein – brushing your teeth – saying your prayers, "Now I lay me down to sleep." – a forty below wind chill just an inch and a half away – frost on the pane – pepper in your nose – ketchup – gravy on everything – boiled potatoes – the Old Man's mood swings – the eavy icicles – the inevitable thaw – the inevitable freeze – the lilac sneeze – the iron ore-y swamps – the northern pike lakes…

The construction site grew so large they hired two more labor dudes. I was head labor dude because I was hired first, that's about all it takes. One of the dudes was Native American from the Pacific Northwest. I asked, "Hey, were you there when Mount St. Helens erupted?" "Yeah, man, there was ash everywhere, it was cool. It was like driving through a blizzard. Except that the ash was so fine it clogged air filters, got into the oil pans and seized-up motors. Yeah, but other than that, it was cool." We became fast friends, both being heavy drinkers. He led me on several tours of his favorite strip clubs. He'd sit there with an ear-to-ear grin, but I couldn't get into it, the girls just depressed me. I had a hard time ignoring real life – couldn't help but think what probably led them there.

In between strip clubs I let Native American in on the HUD situation. He was all for getting the money he deserved.

The other labor dude was practically invisible. Even though he was huge, you could hardly make him out – barely any features except a tiny pair of tinted spectacles so thick they blotted him out. The longer you stared, the less there was to see. We found that it was best to keep him out of the way, so we put him on a high fiber insulation diet, per the local fire code specifications. He spent most days stuffing fire retardant insulation in the walls of a tiny crawl space that ran right down the middle of each townhouse. He'd get himself started with his head in the hole then we'd shove him by the feet until he caught his knees. He'd wiggle in from there, pushing a bale of insulation in front of him and breaking off hunks to fill the gaps.

I got to know some of the guys from the different trades. The plumbers were the most pragmatic about life – pretty much a shit flows downhill philosophy – it was perfectly fitting. They were insatiable alcoholics. Every night after work, without fail, they would polish off a case of beer together before heading home to their apartments – they were all going through divorce. They preferred to keep their official income down until after the divorce settlement, so they worked part-time on the payroll and took cash on the side for everything else.

The electricians considered themselves at the top of the hierarchy. They felt anyone could hammer a nail, or fit a pipe, or paint a wall, but it took real expertise to deal with electricity. They kept to themselves. They held their conversations exclusive. They looked down their noses. Everyone ignored them.

The dry-wallers and carpet layers were mostly crank heads – some were dealers. They were their own best customers – to see those guys move through a building – zip zip zip – they were done. The parade continued when the tapers arrived walking on stilts, "Look what the dry-wallers left behind... Why, it's some dust in a baggy."

The carpenters were the most eclectic group on the construction site. You couldn't pin them down for the most part. Some were loud and stupid like Foreman, while others were philosophers. They could be anything from a high school dropout to a Doctor of Physics. Working side by side – those were some fucked up conversations. Except when it was about the work, then it was all shortcuts and abbreviations – straddling the rafters – obeying the method.

I usually hung out with the painters – cannabis and coffee, that's what they were about. They were always feeling good, freckled in off-white or beige. One of them was a lippy Minnesota Nordic – grew up working-class in South St. Paul – got a chunk of money when his mom died, but given his rather rowdy history, his family (all of them were older) didn't trust that he would spend it well. They suggested he buy a house in that same South St Paul neighborhood and if he could handle that, they'd give him the rest. I told him my condemned house story and he just happened to have a room for rent, "A friend of mine is moving out this weekend. He's gotta spend six months in the pen on a drug related conviction."

I declined to share my situation, "Yeah, well, nobody's perfect."

The room already had a bed, dresser and closet. I shook out the plastic garbage bag on the bed and sorted it out. Painter's girlfriend also lived in the house – she was pretty laid back – trying in vain to settle him down. She hit a rough period when we started using crank. It didn't matter to me – it had no affect – I couldn't catch a buzz. My life was winding down. That wasn't true for Painter. Out on the town he couldn't help himself. He'd slam into walls, tables, chairs, open his big mouth and end up insulting the biggest dude in the joint. Usually by saying something perverted to the big dude's girlfriend. I would have to step in, "Sorry, Big Dude, my friend is really fucked up – besides he's a pussy just look at him – wouldn't do you much good to stomp the loser – I'll get him out of here quick."

I was Painter's guardian angel from one smoked out bar to the next, he hardly noticed, really, he thought I was a drag. "Come on, Mick! Stop being such a goddamn downer. Let's go! There's gotta be someplace we haven't been."

Trippin'

It was Friday after work. I took a road trip down to Mason City with Country because he said, "My cousins are having a big blow-out party, let's fucking go." We got ourselves cleaned up and fed, then we picked up a liter of tequila for the long drive from the Twin Cities. When we arrived we still had a little left, so we sat in the car and slammed down shots from a Styrofoam cup (with a Mountain Dew chaser) until it was gone, then strode fully loaded into their rental.

They had a little thing going – chuckling around a pool table, tipping their brews, holding their cues, landing their blows. Someone piped up, "The big party is just down the street. We can get there on foot." We sort of assembled at the door – we didn't have a leader, we didn't want a leader. We went down an alley, crossed a street, down another alley to another street, a couple of blocks further and there was the party in full swing. I went inside with the others and got lost in a sea of strangers. I bought a cup, pumped a beer and wandered around trying to look like I belonged. There was a parting of the crowd and Country stumbled through, wasted. Some girl walked up and told him to open wide, then she popped a pill in his mouth. He wandered off to hit on a fiancée by the shower curtain while Drug

Pusher turned to me and said, "All I have left is some acid would you like a hit?"

"No doubt about it."

"Follow me." She led me to a room upstairs, dug in a drawer, pulled out a sheet of acid, Mickey Mouse, I believe. She tore one off and held out her hand, "That'll be five dollars."

"Oh, I thought it was free."

"I'm not a fucking charity. Do you want it or not?" I gave her fifteen, dropped three Mickeys on my tongue and headed downstairs.

I got a funny feeling – inside my head or somewhere close by. This would not be the usual trip of happiness and color tracers – this was black, poison. My idea was to dilute the poison with alcohol. I swam through the house, fish diving into every drink. I was in a skirmish with myself. I followed my shadow into the kitchen. There was a guy jamming Van Halen through a twenty watt amp. I hated him. I nudged a dude next to me, "That guy sucks!" The dude yelled out, "Hey, this guy thinks he's better than you!" Guitar guy looked me over. I wasn't that impressive. He decided to make me prove it. He handed over the guitar. I skipped the bullshit and went straight to the finale. I hit the final E and tried to smash the guitar on the kitchen floor. I didn't get past the counter, was mugged in the corn belt and pushed out the back door. They even pulled down the shades.

"I'll say when we're through!" I reached for the nearest object – a trash can lid. I kicked over the can and threw the lid like a Frisbee at the back door. It hooked through a window. I made my way along the side of the house and came in through the front door. I spotted Drug Pusher and started harassing her about the shitty acid she sold me. Then someone yelled, "There's the fucker who broke the window." Five assholes stormed after one asshole. Luckily, one of Country's cousins stepped in. He suggested I go back to the rental and shoved me out the front door.

I didn't need them anyhow – the cold would do – I stumbled forward to the sidewalk – the lights went out – suddenly I didn't know my way around – couldn't remember which alley to take – the wind was a motherfucker – no hat or boots or gloves.

Early spring days bring a thaw. The snow melts and runs over the streets and sidewalks. At night the water freezes and the scene changes. Even when you're sober, it's tough to navigate. The wind and the ice had their way with me. Time and again I hit the ice, got back to my feet, hit it again. I had to crawl to get anywhere. Even then I wasn't sure I was getting anywhere. Was I going backwards or forwards? Am I moving farther away or getting closer? It all looked the same. I put my hands to my ears – I couldn't feel either. I was determined to get out of the goddamn wind. I bumped my way to the side of an apartment building and got a little protection from the wind, but it didn't last. I kept moving along the edge, found a door, a crack, pulled it open, took a few steps down to a hallway, apartment doors, laundry. I stepped in, the dryer was spinning. I crawled under the folding table, curled into a ball. The room grew bigger, then smaller, bigger, then smaller, or maybe it was me changing size. The laundry door opened, a tiny teenage girl entered, stopped. I was gargantuan and easy to spot. I tried to shrink to my normal size, crawled out from under the folding table, held out my hands, stared with giant pupils and said the scariest thing possible, "Don't be afraid." In a moment she was gone. I was instantly doubtful that she had been real. I thought I should get out of there, anyway. I stepped into the hall just as the tiny teenager and her mom were coming down the hall. Her mom said the scariest thing possible, "Can I help you with something?" "No, no, no, I was just leaving."

Back on the street I was soon desperate again, willing to take another chance to get out of the cold. I found another door to another apartment building. It was locked. I tried to kick it in, but couldn't even manage that. I looked toward the parking lot. I skated over on my last breath, hoping to find an unlocked door. All the Pintos,

Gremlins and Vegas were locked up tight. Then, salvation – a brand new Cadillac (still had the little paper license in the rear window) with leather interior. I thanked Gods I didn't believe in, told them I would get around to them someday, then settled down for the night. I wasn't going anywhere. Soon enough, though, that caddie started to spin. It was ebbing and flowing and twisting and turning down some California coastal road. Then it was flying, not a comfortable cruising but a blue angel daring. That's when my guts tore loose. My first shot sprayed the dash and steering wheel. I hit it again. I sat up too quick and made myself dizzier still, poured some on the passenger side dash and floor, spun some more, then, found myself hanging over the headrest. Took several passes at the backseat. Somehow I missed myself completely. I crashed in a heap.

Next morning I felt something pounding. I assumed it was just my head, so reached for my blanket but came up empty. Then I heard muffled screaming. A door opened. It was much clearer, "WHAT THE HELL DID YOU DO TO MY CAR!!?" There was an older woman, maybe forty-five or fifty. She had smoker's lips, kind of pursed and wrinkly. Her eyes were red. She was in tears. Her screaming brought everything back together, that cold fucking wind, that hard fucking ice. I scrambled out of my puke pit, stood, squinted, looked around, spotted my car next to the cousin's rental right across the street. I couldn't believe it.

I asked her for a smoke. I didn't smoke, but I thought, what the hell. She shook out a Marlboro. She was a professional, "I hope you're planning on cleaning up this goddamn mess." She wasn't impressed with my ability to ignore her.

"Got a light?"

She lit me up, then put her hands on her hips (just like the Mom used to do) and yelled as I turned and walked away, "Who the hell are you anyway?"

"I'm just your average, ordinary, everyday sinner."

Just Desserts

Cowboy rang me up one day and said, "We have a court date set for the end of September. You still have the job right?"

"Yes."

"Good, that'll look good to the judge. Don't forget to get a haircut and wear a suit."

"Alright."

I set my sights on starting a HUD investigation before I was locked away for whatever. I called the local HUD number and they put me through to an investigator and he agreed that it was something. We met face to face at a Perkins Restaurant. I gave him the big story while he jotted it down and ate his scrambled eggs.

"They tell us to get lost whenever one of your boys comes around the site. Anyway, do we have a case?"

"Yeah, maybe. You'll have to sign an official complaint and when they find out, they'll probably fire you. There's nothing I can do to help you with that. Are you willing to take that risk?"

"No doubt about it."

The wheels of justice were rolling for and against me. No stopping the bureaucracy now – that's what it was made for, to sally forth and grind up its target.

My court day arrived like a throbbing heartache. I met Cowboy in the courthouse lobby, by the elevators. We shared a ride with the prosecutor to the eighth floor. Cowboy introduced me, "Hey, Jim, this is the kid you're trying to put away." I gave him my best baby face, reached out and shook his hand. "You got yourself a good looking client there, Cowboy."

I sat up front while a few family and friends filtered in to support me – all women. Even my much neglected Swedish Geisha was there – bolt upright on an aisle seat. On the other side of the courtroom sat Chief Moustache, all by himself. He seemed rather amused by the whole affair. He kept eyeballing Swedish Geisha. I sat wishing I'd taken twice as much of his dough.

They adjourned us to the hall and we waited while Cowboy and Prosecutor plea-bargained. The fact that only women had shown up for the hearing, stuck to me. I hadn't done anything good for any of them. I was just another weak man – balance in the negative – they had to deal with. The Old Man didn't show, that wasn't surprising, we left each other long ago. But there was the Mom – all hunkered down on a bench seat – registering at only half-fake sunny. She sat with fingers intertwined, between her mom and her sister, praying for the rebirth of little Mick. Grandma sat there with the usual, "This kid is a dead end road," look on her face or a smile that stretched into a grimace.

Cowboy returned with good news, "Looks like this is your lucky day. Your partner-in-crime, Timmy Tatters', case was settled yesterday and since his family paid back a big chunk of the money, they went light on his punishment. His eighteen months were suspended, he only has to serve thirty days in a work release center and it's the same for you." The women cheered, "Hooray! Our little Mick is saved." Good old Minnesota – the second chance state.

They tromped us back inside where I was to give a deposition. They called me forward, swore me in, sat me in front of the mic. I went easy on myself, made it clear I was confused, had little understanding, just a little greedy, perhaps. I mapped out a general admission. Then Chief Moustache got a chance, he was pissed off, "Your Honor, how can I go back to my employees and tell them that crime doesn't pay?" The judge pointed his finger at me and said, "Clearly, that kid is not the ringleader. I can't give him a longer sentence than Mr. Tatters just because he can't pay you back."

I reported for work release the following week. From the outside it looked like a community college campus, a one layer cake with snow frosting. When I got up close, though, it was another story.

I stood outside waiting for the guy on duty to buzz me in. He wasn't in a hurry. I got the first notion of where I was on the ladder. It was nothing but tough love from here on out. You're on your own in this fucking world. I kicked at the snow and stared up at the trees. There was a tall thin oak with a branch that stuck straight out its side about twenty-five feet off the ground. It was exactly like one that stood in the backyard of the mini-ranch...

I was twelve when I braided up a rope swing out of bailing twine and grabbed the twenty-five foot ladder, trembled my way to the top and tied up an end with half hitches and rabbit knots. I tied the hanging end to an old tire and swung awhile with that. But I was ambitious and impatient, wanted to go higher and higher. I cut the rope, pushed the tire out of the way and hung on like Tarzan to a knotted up end. I created a launch pad by wheeling a hay wagon into position. I climbed aboard with knot in hand and stood at the edge and jumped – not bad. I rolled an old wire spool onto the hay wagon and set it on end and jumped from there – better yet! I raided the Mom's kitchen for a lemony plastic chair and placed it on top of the wire spool – magnificent! On the plastic chair I stacked our set of 1959 Encyclopedia Britannica. I clenched the rope in my teeth and made my way up through the alphabetic ages. I wobbled at the top and jumped as ancient civilization collapsed beneath me. I wrapped my legs over the knot and swung down and out. I cleared the roof line. I measured the moon with my big toe. Then the rope snapped. It had worn through at the branch and let go. I came down, still squeezing the knot, and landed flat on my back, knocking the wind out of me. I laid there gasping like a fish dangling from one of my barbed hooks. Poor thing, I thought, I'll never fish again, or anything else for that matter. Little Sister walked up holding three kittens, "Look what I found." She was smiling. The big burning sun winked at me from over her shoulder. I sucked in a mouthful of air and let go. Little Sister held her kittens close and ran for the kitchen. She brought back the Mom and by then I was bent over my knees. The Mom looked me over and shook her head, "I told you that was a bad idea."…

The guard finally buzzed me in, patted me down, read me the riot act. I served my sentence with chronic drunk drivers, a cocaine addict who held up a Brinks truck with a pencil and a heavy metal rocker busted with a little bag of weed (for the second time). It was eighty-five percent blue collar white. Most of the members were older, most of them were no wiser, most of them were still tumbling downward.

Our little work release prison had a lunch room, an office and where they kept us they called pods. Don't look to the sky for the pod people, we are the pod people. Each pod had a lounge with a TV surrounded by a dozen cells. We bunked five to a cell. It was lights out at nine-thirty. We stayed up late laughing at each other's sad stories.

Once a week the guards made us clean up in a hurry, "Come on prisoners – move it, move it, move it! Let's get those beds made. Make it tight, prisoner! Someone needs to scrub those sinks and those toilets. Now! You don't wanna lose your privileges do ya?" We'd run around trying to look busy, but the truth was, there were so many of us serving time, we mostly just got in each other's way.

A couple days before Thanksgiving weekend the prison brass announced that we could all spend the holiday at home with our families, or wherever, as long as we reported back there by noon on Sunday. "And you better not come back intoxicated. We'll be giving everyone the breathalyzer and any who fail will end up over in County."

Too many friends found out I was getting out for the holiday. Everybody made plans. I enjoyed a six pack after work with the plumbers, smoked a bowl with Painter, drank a bottle with Country before he headed up North to his parents, pawed Swedish Geisha for an hour, dropped her off early, picked up a short term thing, took her to a little pub where we met up with Painter, his girlfriend, and a neighbor friend. We were stupid drunk.

Short Term Thing was so hot blooded. We'd fucked a few times before. She was alright, but she miscalculated her worth to me. I was having a very important drunken discussion with Painter – she felt I was ignoring her. She tried to make me jealous by hanging all over Neighbor. He was enjoying it, why ruin it for everyone. The more I ignored her, the more ridiculous the display. She stormed front and center, "I'm with, Neighbor, now, so don't even bother talking to me. I'm through with you and I don't want to ever talk, or see, or speak, or look at, or say anything, 'cause I'm through with you now." She lost her train, looked up at the ceiling trying to focus in the dim light, found it, sort of, came back swinging, "Did you know I'm with Neighbor now?" I gave her a big yawn and looked over her head, "Yeah, I already heard."

"Well, what're you're gonna do about it? Don't you see I love you? I'll never leave you, Mick, never."

"That's what I'm afraid of."

"You fucking asshole! I'm through with you now and I don't want to ever talk, or see, or speak, or look at, or say anything, because I'm through with you now."

By the end of the night, Short Term Thing came seeking solace. She followed me out the door and pulled up next to me. I didn't turn my head, "What happened to Neighbor? I thought you were going home with him?" She laughed, "Oh, you're so silly. I was just upset because you were being naughty. Anyway, that's ancient history. Where are we going?"

"Nowhere, I suppose."

The next day, Painter's Girlfriend made a Thanksgiving turkey while we watched a football game, snorted a little crank, drank a few cases of beer, ended the evening in a wrestling match, me vs. Painter on the kitchen floor. His girlfriend refereed, reluctantly. Painter was so goddamn skinny, it was easy throwing him off into a corner where Referee jumped in and gave him a ten count lecture. The door bell rang. Referee got it. It was Neighbor. He stepped through, looked us over and said, "You two at it again?"

I looked at Painter, "We have a history? Together?"

Neighbor continued, "Hey, Mick, I hope I'm not being insensitive here, but would it be possible for me to get Short Term Thing's number?"

"Gee, I don't know, Neighbor, I'm still fucking her."

"Really?" He turned to Painter, "Did you see the way she was hanging all over me last night?" He came back to me, "She said she was through with you now and she didn't want to ever talk, or see, or speak, or look at, or say anything to you, because she was through with you."

"Yeah, she's a weird fucking lover."

There was no shaking him off. He was convinced he adored her and she adored him. So I put her up for bid, "Hey, Neighbor, what's your offer?"

"Pardon?"

"I can't give her up for nothing."

He hemmed and he hawed. That seemed silly, not at all gentlemanly, "I'll give ya five bucks."

"Not even close, my friend, that's some prime real estate right there."

"All I got is a twenty."

"That's just not gonna do. You'll need to go further. She's so fucking tight."

"I've got some hockey tickets for a game in December – the Penguins – Mario Lemieux."

"Yeah, if he's healthy. Where are they located?"

"Lower level."

"How many?"

"Four, but you can have two."

"Hey, Painter, you wanna see the North Stars play the Penguins?"

"Sure."

"Alright, give me two tickets and the twenty." I handed him Short Term Thing's number, "Are you sure you wanna do this?" Of course he did. What the hell were a couple tickets and twenty dollars? He was still going to the game. She could be the one he'll marry.

The next night, Painter threw a little party. Neighbor was there. In walked Short Term Thing. She didn't remember him, he got all droopy. I felt bad for him, so poured twenty dollars worth of booze down his gullet and tried to convince Short Term Thing to give him a quick screw. "Are you fucking kidding!?!" It was no use, he faded toward the door. When no one was looking he went home. We continued without him, got seriously loaded, argued about motorcycles, shook our heads over the football team, made passes at each other's girlfriends. It was just another lost weekend.

Sunday at noon I was back at the work release center and obediently assembled with all the others outside the prison. It was frigid. They made us wait an extra forty-five minutes just to get us back in the mood. Eventually, the doors opened. We formed a line, signed-in and blew into the breathalyzer. Four or five guys were sent over to County because they couldn't resist a drink on the way in.

We stretched out on our bunks as usual – lights out – talking about our rowdy weekends. Heavy Metal Rocker began talking about his sentence reduction due to his good behavior. I laughed, "Are you kidding me? I thought that was a Hollywood invention."

"Hey, Mick, don't you know anything? Everyone gets time off for good behavior."

"What's the deduction so far on my sentence?"

"When did you get in?"

"November 1st."

"Dude, your last day should have been this past Friday."

"What!? Don't fuck with me, here."

"I'm not fucking with ya. On a thirty day sentence, you only serve twenty-five days."

I didn't want to spend another second in that fucking joint. Why didn't anybody tell me? Time off for good behavior!? I ran to the guard at the front desk, "Excuse me, sir, there's been a mistake. I'm not supposed to be here – should have gotten out of here last Friday. Please check your records." He wasn't concerned. He didn't move a muscle. He was thick with condescension, "When we get an order to release you, we will release you. Go back to your pod."

I stomped back to my cell, indignant, such a travesty. Was there no justice in the world? I got Cowboy on the phone. I rang him up at home, "I've been informed that I should be out of this fucking place. Something about time off for good behavior. I haven't had any infractions, how come they're not letting me out?"

"Oh, ah, you gotta put in for that," adding, "Now, I can't promise you anything, but I'll try to get you out of there by tomorrow evening."

I was released three days later, Wednesday 9:33 p.m., day 30. I said goodbye to my work release gang. Most of them were in for much longer, poor fucking repeat offenders. That wasn't going to be me – no way. The easiest incarceration was enough.

Minnesota Hockey Night

Hockey night arrived. We clamored over to a South St. Paul bar. Driving to the game is a great big hassle so a few of the local bars and taverns get together and rent a school bus and driver for the night, throw in a sixteen gallon keg and charge ten dollars – there and back – all the beer you can hammer. The bus driver drops you off and picks you up right at the door. That meant everyone could get extra loaded and we did. "There'll be lots of beer on the bus so let's do shots here," Painter said.

The ride over was a lot like the seventh grade, except for the beer. We threw it down our throats, at each other, out the window. The bus turned into a giant Popsicle. It was a stiff ride. We bumped our heads on the ceiling. Sometimes we landed in the aisle, plenty of beer there too. We conspired to keep each other down with salt-bottomed boots and shoes. Friends and strangers dished it out equally to each other, you couldn't tell who was on your side. The best bet was no one.

By the time we arrived we were violently happy, in the beginning then all that booze caught up. Luckily the North Stars scored first! Hooray! Stupid drunk white guys attempting high fives only managed to slap each other in the face. It got better from there. Lemieux scored twice in thirty seconds and our guy Dino Cicarelli was knocked to the ice. The benches cleared, so did the stands. We rushed the glass, threw every conceivable object, including someone's underwear freshly ripped from its socket. The refs called the game early. That caused a bigger riot. Painter caught a Rodney-round-house right to the head. He went down and out. Neighbor and I carried him out of there sideways, bumping him along the ground, as usual. On the way back in the bus he came to and smiled. It was another successful Minnesota hockey night.

Born to be a Minor Thing

They brought down the hammer at the construction site. The general contractor was aware of the HUD investigation and someone had to pay. I was seen as the instigator, I couldn't disagree. I said so long to the labor dudes and went home to my rented room in Painter's house.

My HUD guy got me on the phone a few days later. Yes, indeed, the general contractor was guilty of something and HUD Guy would get to the bottom of it. He setup a meeting between the general contractor and us. We sat around a conference table. General Contractor was angry, he furrowed his brow at me. He'd pay the other guys but he wouldn't pay me. He tried to claim that I was a supervisor, so I fell under the umbrella of management and was entitled to nothing. We argued back and forth. HUD guy didn't help much. The labor dudes were worse, they still worked for General Contractor. They were getting theirs so they didn't want to get involved.

General Contractor leaned forward, "I'll give you the pay difference, but for only half your hours." I chewed my tongue and wondered why he got to demand the sentence, let alone even be sitting there? He was caught stealing five times the amount I was, but there he was telling me what he'd do. I wanted to wring his chicken neck.

His greed and devilry reminded me of the Old Man back in the old days when he was squeezing his one dollar bills. He had them rubber-banded in the sock drawer. When he'd banded a thousand, he traded them for a custom-made saddle. He went all the way to Miles City, Montana to get it. It was a no frills workingman's saddle, he said. He spent all winter in front of the TV playing John Wayne westerns – rubbing it with an oily rag, lovingly, on a news-papered floor. "Oh, those were the days," he would say, "when a man could get a little dirt under his nails, ride on for days." To where he never said.

I never asked. I stood off to the side and inched my way back to my room to listen to a tape of "Foghat Live" that Neighbor kid had given me during his James Taylor phase when he rode his shifting sands of attention through the first verse of over a hundred songs on an acoustic guitar his brother had given him. He'd punch through a verse, stop, make an observation, plunk a few strings, break into the first verse of another song, stop, make another observation, plunk a few strings and so on and so forth. He was too nervous for focus. He enjoyed quantity over quality. He didn't have time for any refined sort of taste, kept a worry list under his pillow, slept in the attic then moved to the basement. We'd get high and make giggle tapes with north woods profundity and guitars interlaced.

Neighbor Kid was scared to death of the Old Man, couldn't see how I could take it. When cornered, he called him "sir" and got the hell out of there. One waning September summer day he happened by on the way back from somewhere, peered through my window and woke me from an infected trance. "Hey, Mick, what have you been up to?" I didn't bother to get up, but mumbled something through the window screen. He lit a cigarette and went on talking. Then we heard the roar of the Old Man's motor from a couple miles away, the constant revving, downshifting through the corners, rubbing the edges off the tires. There was no one else like him. He was coming on fast. Neighbor kid jumped out of his sneakers, stamped out his cigarette and ducked behind a tree before the Old Man hit the driveway in his company pickup truck, courtesy of Inter City Natural Gas. He got free mileage and gasoline. He used it on nights, weekends and holidays for personal things like dump runs, firewood collections, hauling lumber, straw bales for bedding the stalls for the horses, and dropping us off at church in our Sunday worst.

Big Sister and I rode in the back, in the open air, year round. The Old Man and the Mom sat in front with Little Sister tucked in between. The best present we got one year was a plexi-glass topper installed over the truck bed. We still didn't have a heater. We were told that it was better than nothing. We couldn't disagree...

My labor dudes white knuckled the edge of the table with a faraway look in their eyes, way past the oak table, to the end of this here uncomfortable mess. I led them to the edge of this tabletop and here they abandoned me. What was the use? Everyone was against me. I looked them over with sore eyes, they fell into slow motion. Everything General Contractor said was fine by them. Poor things couldn't even look at me. HUD guy clearly did not want a confrontation. He leaned toward General Contractor with a reassuring grin, eyes swinging between us like a shark tail. General Contractor was the saddest one of all, so well off for so long, he wasn't used to losing, especially to some blue collar slob. He'd left his tired wife waiting in the car, "I'll keep it running dear, this won't take long."

He pushed himself forward, fists clenched, winning was it. The money hardly mattered anymore. I counter offered, "Give me seventy percent and we're done here." General Contractor jumped up and stuck out his hand, "You got yourself a deal."

Unemployment Benefits

I went down to the unemployment office to apply for benefits. They put me through the paces, "In order to qualify for your weekly benefit you'll have to make an honest work search effort. You will have to fill out this form, every week. You must enter three different company contacts. You may be audited, so tell the truth. We don't pay the first week, we gotta check up on you first. You can call in your claim beginning on Sunday for the week ending. If your claim is approved, we will send you the money, a little bit each time. Too much might overwhelm you. You need a babysitter, that's why we're here. You gotta work. Freedom isn't free. Oh sure, we'd all love to sit around and do nothing, but not here, not on our watch anyway."

They offered classes: "How To Fill Out a Job Application Form," "Resume Writing: Do's and Don'ts," "Interview Techniques 101." They bribed you into taking them by counting it as a job contact. I stayed away.

Every week I selected my contacts randomly from the want ads or the phone book, whatever. I spent most of elementary school standing in the hall so I was used to bucking the system. I was betting that I wouldn't be audited, because I was sure they didn't have the manpower to get to a fraction of us, and they simply didn't care.

The place was a morgue, an un-motivating mess. The system dictated everything. If it isn't signed and notarized twice, the computer just might reject it. If that happened, they'd send it to accounting where someone would hand deliver it to the garbage. Then you'll have to start over on an alternate form and don't forget to fill out the twenty-page special addendum. Be thorough, Little Boy, dot every fucking "i". If the computer chokes again you'll be disqualified. You'll soon see what it's like at the bottom of the richest country on the planet. It's just like the third world. Is that motivation enough for you to keep Christmas holy? Screw the other guy, buy low sell high, exploit a niche, pan for gold, play the lottery.

It was a job just to get my benefits. I stayed on until the end and took every last red cent.

Nonchalant

I fell into a routine – up by noon – wander across the street to the gas station for a newspaper, chips and a Mello Yello. Back at the house – the easy chair – turn down the TV – turn up the stereo – fish a roach out of the ashtray – sip the can – chew the chips – sit until evening – clean up – look for a party.

I was sinking low again – the days bled together – I couldn't remember a thing. Whenever I did some crank it only got me to level. I stopped looking for parties. I could barely tolerate the ones that came to me. My friends were less friendly (or maybe it was me) they seemed to have hardened in their opinions of things. Maybe it's the long cold winters and no time to hibernate. That's what I needed; a good long sleep. I no longer played the blame game with them. They no longer bounced anything off me. They began to pair off – sat close in the pickup or sedan, shared the same side of the booth, bought little gray houses and popped out little gray versions of themselves. The end was here.

I approached my probation officer with a sudden desire to leave the state of Minnesota. Big Sister was living in Seattle and talking it up as great place for a new start. Probation Officer was a dip-shit sadist, "You must pay your restitution on time, every time, even though you've been laid off. Pucker your asshole when I'm speaking to you! That doesn't mean you can stop paying your restitution. Whether you collect unemployment, or not, you still have to pay, you little jag off. As far as moving to Washington state, I don't know, it wouldn't be up to me. Bend over so I can swat your behind. And remember, you cannot leave the state for any reason without written permission. You see, the rules must be obeyed. Haven't you learned that yet? Has it absorbed itself into that mediocre brain of yours? You simply must put it in a letter. Is this a turn for the better? How have you changed your ways? Suck my cock, give examples, you'll need at least fifteen copies, submit them to me in one hour. And again, it's not up to me."

I set about writing the greatest letter of appeasement. I'd been writing it my entire life – here it would all come together. I threw God in the mix every chance I could. If it pleases your Honor, your worthiness, your boner, indeed, the Lord does now guide me through these troubled waters. May I rise above, your Honor, may I rise above. I know now that only through God and hard work will I ever be able to repay the debt that I owe you. Say, mind if I hit the Pacific coast for awhile? Out of your hair, so to speak. If I fall off the wagon, better there than here, right? Come on, why ya wanna hang on to a felon? I got a letter from Big Sister. She's living there, now. She has promised to watch over me. She's not a criminal, your Honor.

I walked around acting like my move to Seattle was a done deal, "Hey everybody, I'm temporary. Take a good look because next week, I'll be gone and you won't see me anymore."

Friends who had known me since grade school scoffed, "Hey, Mick, do you remember saying that before every summer vacation back in grade school? And sure enough, there you were the next school year, wiping your snot on the bottom of your desk. Yeah, we saw ya."

It was true, every winter the Old Man would work himself into a red hot ember, "Goddamn it! This is it. We're getting the hell out of here next summer. That's right, goddamn it, we're moving to Montana. There is no goddamn doubt about it." Kindergarten through 4th grade I delivered to my brethren my own version of the great beyond, "Gather round heathens of the North. I told the Old Man that it's time to get out of this damn place. We're gonna buy a ranch in Montana and I'm gonna be a cowboy." Returning for the new school year was a grand humiliation. My friends would attack and jeer and box my ears and that set the whole bad year in motion.

I got Country on the phone one day, "Hey, Country, how about rolling west with me when I get the word? I hear the Pacific Northwest is awesome, better than this fucking place anyway."

"Hey, Mick, ya stupid son of a bitch, you don't get it. I love it here – all the hunting, fishing, snowmobiling, it's fucking great. Besides, I just bought ten acres on the lake. I'll have a house up in no time – I'll build it myself. And every night I'll walk out to the end of my dock and enjoy the peace and quiet. So don't count on me from here on out."

Michael McDaeth

My Pacino

I spent a few long weekends at the mini-ranch. The Old Man was in one of his silent periods and the Mom stood to the side, stirring the gravy or chocolate pudding (the Old Man's favorite) hoping one of her concoctions would break the silence. Winter set in early with a terrible cold snap, but no snow. The frost sank deep into the ground and the ice froze thick on the lakes, smooth as glass. I bought a pair of hockey skates and skated around and around on the clear ice.

The grandparents decided to spend Christmas in Minnesota. It was nearly five years, now, since I had pushed Gramps down the freeway to Texas. They drove up in their white Cadillac. Grandma pointed the way, "North, you old fool, north."

They pulled up the driveway, got out, stretched themselves. Then Gramps had a heart attack. The holiday turned black with worst case scenarios then, gray, as things improved and finally a bright white when Gramps got out of bed on Christmas morning. A week later, in rang the New Year and it was about time for the grandparents to get back home to Texas. Gramps' heart was too weak for the long drive so he called me over to the easy chair, "Hey kid, they won't let me drive back to Texas, so we're gonna fly. We need some help getting the white Cadillac down there. What're you doing next week?"

"Nothing that can't wait, I suppose."

"Good. We'll give you a few hundred for helping out, alright?"

"You don't need to do that, and I'm serious this time."

"We'll talk about that later."

The next week I was all dressed up in the white Cadillac with an envelope of cash for expenses. I planned a side trip through El Paso to visit St. Olaf, who was living there now. I drove through the day and night, running in the high nineties at regular intervals. The road blurred at first, but I got used to it. I rolled along while the state signs came and went – Iowa, Missouri, Kansas. The landscape was endless, windswept, frozen ground. I entered Oklahoma, hit a snowstorm and plunged through four foot drifts, then followed a snowplow up a motel exit. I sat in a lonely room for three days while it blew and piled up outside. I couldn't sleep, the road just kept coming on, coming on, coming on, under my eyelids.

The layover put a big dent in the envelope. It would be tight the rest of the way.

Day four in Oklahoma City and the temperature climbed out of the basement. The snow beat a hasty retreat and I was in Texas by midmorning. South to Fort Worth, then west-southwest through West Texas and its huge gaps between towns – dust clouds on the horizon, little mountain chains, fields of oily grasshoppers, flaming refineries, rows of holding tanks, massive power lines. I drove through a torched sunset and into the dark, hurling myself along. No money for a motel, just gas and chips through the dreamy night. Deep into the black morning, me, droopy eyed, yawning in the clipping-along nineties. Suddenly, an explosion of fire and light and the vague outline of a burning truck flashed in my head, then it was gone. The sky was clear as far as I could see, but the image brought me to attention and put a sudden fear in my gut. I pulled my foot from the gas and took it down to seventy as I was coming over a rise to a dip in the road. Awake like the beginning of the day – something black in the road, blacker than the pavement. No time to squint and consider, I swerved on instinct to miss the black ghost, zipped along in the oncoming lane still going seventy. I swung my head wide and saw a truck being pushed off the road by people lined up along the taillights. Was it the same truck? I don't know, but it was close enough. There was a tingling up my spine and then, such a buzzing in my skull, I thought an artery had burst in my head.

My worst nightmare was dying from a hemorrhaging brain ever since a good pal and fishing buddy had a brain aneurysm on a fishing dock on Big Sandy lake. He was only twelve years old when he collapsed and died while reeling in a tiny perch. The perch was still on the line when they found him a few hours later. His parents had the tiny perch stuffed and lacquered and embedded in the tombstone with the words, 'HERE LIES "LITTLE" MAC MC CONKEY. HE LOVED TO FISH.'

Daylight arrived deep in West Texas. Exhausted, I pulled off, walked to the edge of the Pecos and fought the urge to throw the keys to the white Cadillac into the river. The feeling was overwhelming. I don't know what kept me from doing it. It seemed possible, even inevitable, if I were to keep standing there. It was horrible and wonderful, a voice in my head telling me to throw them in, see if you can hit the middle, you'll never know if you don't try. I ran back to the white Cadillac and took off down the road, but I had the same problem.

Driving was easy, fighting the urge to steer into oncoming traffic, or the ditch for that matter, was difficult. What would it be like? How would it turn out for me or them? I drove just over the line, unrolling the probable accident scenes in my head. From impact to funeral, from death bed to wheel chair to limping cane, the awful endless endings. I spied my wallet on the seat next to me, I wanted so much to roll down the window and throw it out. I soaked in the thought of it. Where would it end up? Would I ever get it back? I imagined the moments after I'd let it fly, in a sudden panic, pulling off and backtracking, cussing in the ditch what a stupid son of a bitch I was, and so forth.

A few more miles and the white Cadillac sputtered and hiccupped and slowed and slowed and slowed until I was barely going fifteen with the pedal floored. It was in the middle of nowhere. My salty eyes strained the horizon for a savior while my bleeding mind painted a terrible picture of the road ahead and no money to pay for it. I stroked the dash and pleaded with the white Cadillac, "Not here, sweetheart, let's just keep it going until we find something better." I pulled to the side and crawled along the gravel strip inching toward nothing, coming from nowhere. Finally, I saw a road sign advertising a gas station twenty-five miles ahead. I kept stroking the dash, "Come on baby." I kept my foot to the floor and my brain on hemorrhage and I willed the white beast the twenty-five-and-three-tenths miles and, oh, what a lovely sight – a beacon on top of a ramp with the Texas flag waving in a twenty knot breeze. There was a greasy mechanic on duty. He was the best looking guy in Texas. He went straight to the problem, popped the hood, unscrewed the gas filter, held it to the light then put it to his mouth and blew. It was plugged solid except for a pinhole, a pinhole that got me there. "This here cheap gas filter is what's the problem. Been seein' a lot of this lately. It's not genuine GM." He screwed in a new one and the white Cadillac came back to its full five-hundred-cubic-inch life. "Let's see, here, that'll be twenty dollars for parts and labor."

After paying the bill, and filling the tank, that was it for the envelope money. I took it nice and slow the rest of the way to El Paso. I coasted down into the valley with the white Cadillac in neutral and made it to St. Olaf's apartment with a half tank left on the gauge. St. Olaf was home from work and smoking a joint of Texas ditch weed –

weak, weak stuff. He was no longer with Spring Quarter. She lived in Houston with the kid. He shared the apartment with his new girlfriend. Most of her family lived just over the border in Juarez. She was shy and sweet and believed in the devil he was fighting.

St. Olaf and his girlfriend took me out on the town. After smoking a couple weak joints, we poured some drinks, then I had a few more on my own and there I was grinning my fucked-up grin about something stupid, as usual, when a girl walked up and said, "My Pacino, my Pacino." Was she Italian? Did she think I was Italian? I couldn't tell. Oh, but I was smashed in that fucking place when she asked me for a light and gave me that straight look in the eye like I knew what she was thinking. St. Olaf leaned over, "Hey, we're gonna take off are you coming?" Possessive answered for me without breaking her stare, "I'll take good care of my Pacino."

She dropped me back at St. Olaf's place so I could pick up the white Cadillac and I don't know how I followed her to her place, but she kept me behind with a bump and grind, waving her panties in the rearview mirror. We pulled into her apartment complex and filled two slots next to each other. I rammed it into Park at ten miles an hour (what a disgrace for a country boy) and dropped the keys on the floor. Suddenly, a voice in my head was screaming, "Get the fuck out of here!" But she caught me before I could get the key back in the ignition. She pulled me out of the car, grabbed me by the belt buckle, threw me over her shoulder, carried me upstairs somewhere, dumped me on the couch. She handed me a beer, all the while giving me that straight ahead stare. She was yet another single parent, dirt fucking poor, shit fucking job. I think she was a part-time stripper. I kept sliding off the couch. She suggested her bed would be better. I couldn't disagree. I followed, as usual, and fell in. She climbed on top, slipped it in and said, "My Pacino my Pacino, I knew I was going to fuck you when I first saw you, remember? You couldn't find your lighter. I knew right then I'd be fucking you like this." She bucked herself off and put it in her mouth, tongued the shaft, "Oh, my Pacino, have you been fucking someone else? I can taste her pussy. It's a good thing I'm not the jealous type, huh?" At the end of each sentence she gave it a little extra something, "I'm gonna make you forget all about her, my Pacino." She climbed back on top and fucked up a storm. She gave me such a beating I couldn't come. She kept me pinned to the mattress and again with her straight ahead stare, "You've never been fucked like this before have you, my Pacino?" She was right about that, even in my train wrecked condition I could feel her expertise. She pulled right out to the tip, swirled her hips, plunged back down and took it to the bottom, throwing in little off-rhythm thrusts. "Ooohh, my Pacino you're getting it good today aren't you? Can you remember her name? The girl you fucked just before me. The bitch can't fuck you like me, can she my Pacino?"

The next morning I tried to climb out of bed, but Possessive kept pulling me back, "Where are you going? What's the hurry? Let's go out and get some breakfast, I'm starving."

"Nothing doing, I've got to get back to St. Olaf's apartment. We're going to wrestle with the devil."

"When will I see you again?"

"I'll only be in town for a few days."

"I'll entertain you while you're here – no big deal," she gave me a squeeze, "maybe you'll decide to stay longer, huh, my Pacino?"

"Sounds good to me, I'll give you a call, what's your number?" She scrawled it out on a piece of paper. I tried to look interested, read it back to her to prove it. Then I flew out of there and back to St. Olaf's apartment and crashed on the couch.

Just a few hours later Possessive came to the door. I was sleeping. She tried the knob, then banged on the number. Her pounding snapped me out of my twilight condition. I tiptoed to the door, took a peep out the peep hole, and there was my Latin American whore. She felt my shadow through the hollow core, she stepped towards it, there was no escape. I cracked the door and acted all put out and sore. That didn't deter her, she forced entry and took a quick look around. She was worse than the fucking police. She began interrogating me, "You said you were gonna call me. Why haven't you called me?"

"It's only been a few hours, are you fucking kidding me?"

She paused, caught hold of herself and instantly softened, "Oh I'm just kidding. I was in the neighborhood and I saw the white Cadillac so I just thought I'd say hello and give you a little something." She dropped her eyes towards my fly, reached out and helped herself, "I'm just gonna blow you then I'll be on my way." She blew me all right but she didn't leave. Several hours later I had to push her out the door.

"Listen, St. Olaf will be here any minute and the devil will be with him. It's an epic battle you don't want to know about. I'm doing you a favor here."

She said with a frown, "I'll be back later."

St. Olaf and I stayed up late smoking his weak joints and drinking his cheap beer and arguing about the devil. "Listen, St. Olaf, there are a lot of demons out there, I'll give you that, but they're manmade demons. Come on, an all-powerful devil collecting souls? Now that's a bit much."

"Mick! Look at your own life. The devil's been with you every step of the way, talking you into all that crap. I know it."

"I chose to do those things."

"The devil put that thought in your head. I'm telling you, Mick, you're powerless to see the truth. I mean, you're a damn thief and you act like you've done nothing wrong. That's the devil working inside of you."

"I believe that it's okay to steal from big corporations and the government, simply because they are stealing from you, me and everyone else. It was my duty to fight back."

"Mick, that's just more devil talk."

"The truth is, I won't steal again, St. Olaf. The devil being here or not has nothing to do with what I did or what I'll do."

"The devil has many guises. I can barely keep up with him myself and you're weak, Mick. I'm going to pray that the devil doesn't lead you astray again."

"Alright, St. Olaf, thanks."

Next day, Possessive was back at the door but I wouldn't let her in this time, so she left, then returned several more times, slipping notes under the door, "Where are you Pendejo! You can't duck me. I see the white Cadillac in the parking lot."

I had to get out of there, no telling how far she'd go. St. Olaf lent me the gas and food money I needed and said, "Hey, Mick, watch out for the devil. He's everywhere and he never gives up."

Smoothing Everything Over

I got word that the state of Washington was willing to take me on as a client. I began to organize my things. Painter suggested that I rent a U-Haul trailer, but the cost one-way was enough to buy my own, so I had a trailer hitch installed on my car. I checked the paper for used trailers. I found one close by; it looked to be in rough shape. The owner assured me it was road worthy. Still, I had to ask, "I'm moving to Seattle. Will this make the trip?"

"Of course, my newest, dearest friend. She doesn't look it, but she'll follow right along after, no problem."

Such a kindly looking trailer man, I thought to myself, as he was fixing the wiring for the taillights because they had shorted-out before I had even given him the cash.

He covered up nicely, "Golly, that's never happened before. These lights have always worked like a charm. Tell you what, since you didn't dicker on the price, I'm gonna fix 'em if I have to stay out here all night." Trailer Man had such manners and was so charming, certainly another pillar in the community.

I pulled the trailer back to Painter's house and filled it with my loose ends and hauled ass out of there. I was heading up North again – probably for the last time. Before long, I heard a sound. It was coming from the trailer "pffft – pffft – pffft – pffft," a steady rhythm. It followed my lead. The faster I drove, the quicker the beat. I pulled off, got out and walked around the trailer like I was Arkansas Zig Zag way back when. There was definitely a smell like something burning. Nothing I could do about it anyway, so I climbed back in and played a slow waltz the rest of the way, thinking of the money I'd spent on the fucking thing and it might not even make it the measly one hundred twenty miles to the mini-ranch. I asked the ditch weeds, "Such a dreary road I'm on, but what am I suppose to do?" The ditch weeds would not confirm or deny my existence. I took it as it's up to you.

I pulled the trailer down the long gravel driveway with a weeble and a wobble and parked it under a tree. The Old Man came out to inspect it. I told him to leave it alone, but he wouldn't leave it alone. He got up under there with a flashlight, "Ah, here's the problem," pointing between the tire and the trailer bed, "the tire was rubbing against the side of the trailer. You're lucky it didn't blow out and kill ya. That axle is so old it can't take the weight of even your lightweight crap. You were ripped off. Hee hee hee."

"I knew that after a couple miles. I didn't need a flashlight."

The Old Man and I were forever at odds and the Mom ping-ponged between us. She was passive-passive, wandering the house in a nightgown and slippers, holding a cup of coffee with both hands. "Just warming them up," she would say. She was always cold and arthritic yet she followed the Old Man to northern Minnesota, laying eggs by the side of the road, always looking forward well beyond the horizon for things to improve, get better, maybe.

She dove into her religion, made quilts for the Africans, sang out in the church choir – never at home. Just more patience, that's all, just be more patient, all will be resolved, "Let's not act upon this right now, the timing isn't right." Shortly after I was born she fell into the twenty-seven-year depression that would claim her life. Oh, the faint heart of a daughter of an alcoholic father. She shivered like a mouse inside her little hole in the wall, smoothing everything over, regarding the Old Man and his demonic possession, pleading for compromise from her children. Don't stir it up, hold on one more day, better things were ahead as sure as worse things lay behind. Her hands wedged together in a terminal prayer – the blood squeezed out of them. Nothing to take up the space left behind just hollow passageways to wander, hopelessly hopeful.

I worked on her over the years, part-time, tried to give her a boost, hoping she'd leave the Old Man and take us with her. Mostly, I dished it out plain and simple and laid it at her limp feet, like our proud cat bringing its first mouse of the summer into the house. Trouble was, he didn't kill it and the mouse dragged itself away, crawled up into a piece of under-stuffed furniture, and died. I was a mute nine-year-old. I didn't mention it to anybody. A couple days later the Old Man followed his Irish potato nose to the exact spot where the mouse died, took out his Buck knife (from a little leather holster attached to his belt), cut a hole in the fabric and pulled out the putrid carcass. He handed it to me by the tail, "Throw this goddamn thing into the woods and bring me back a stick. I'm gonna teach you to keep the goddamn cat outside."

When the Old Man came at me with the stick, there was no escape but to jump and cry as he swung around my outstretched defending hand to give me the first shot. I made it difficult, he made it more difficult. I couldn't help myself, I had a natural tendency to ward off evil. I went into a hop – all that rabbit fear I guess – he was a bloody red fox. It continued until the demon was satisfied. Then he retired to the living room and sat in front of the TV in a temporary ceasefire.

Eventually, the Old Man called me out of my rabbit hole with the most god-awful, friendly, threatening hustle, "Hey, Mick, get out here the game is on... Goddamn it, get out here!" I barely appeared.

"Hey, where ya been? Jump up on the couch there, and watch the game with me." He stared me down, "Stop the damn pouting will ya? It'll toughen you up a little so no one pushes you around later in life. It's for your own good, goddamn it. So give me a smile and forget about it. It's in the past. Let's just watch the game, our team is ahead, isn't that great?"

Over the years, the Old Man either, pissed and moaned about the entire world, starting with the government, or he sat in vast silent periods, cracking nuts with his bare hands, slurping his Oolong tea, cutting tremendous gassy farts. For months at a time he was out of commission on the couch or lying in bed. He wouldn't let out a peep to anyone except the Mom and even then, it was barely a mumble. It was usually something about me that ailed him.

The Mom begged me to reform my ways. I refused. The Old Man and his demon sank deep down in the seat and looked beyond my passing profile to more tolerable things. We didn't say goodbye, we didn't say anything, the years just piled on. Whenever he popped out of his shell, I'd punch a random series of his buttons, sending him back into solitary confinement. To pass the time, I'd whack tennis balls off the barn wall. The balls would bounce in the horseshit. Eventually, all the balls turned brown. Every time the ball hit the barn it left a shit print, nice and round. After ten thousand strokes the whole side of the wall was practically covered, so I aimed for the gaps in the brown. I was an artist. The acidic horseshit gathered on my tennis racquet and ate away the strings. Eventually they snapped and that was that...

The trailer axle turned out to be from a Model A Ford. I pulled it out back and parked it next to all the other crap the Old Man was going to put up for auction someday. I found another trailer for sale in the paper. I had to drive all the way back down to Minneapolis to see it. The seller had at least twenty of them, custom made, very stout – same fucking price as the Model A axle.

Since I was in town I gave Swedish Geisha a call. It was getting late, we both could tell. She offered me her couch, I said I'd take her to dinner. She was dolled up, but playing it very cool. After dinner we shared some drinks in the lounge, then a few more. We drove back to her place and I followed her upstairs. She changed into a night shirt and, oh, those long smooth legs. We fucked in her beloved missionary position. She whispered, "Don't forget me" then, "don't pull out." I didn't.

I took my sweet time driving back up north. I took highway 169, crisscrossed the Rum River, rode the west bank of Mille Lacs Lake, passed the Indian Reservation for the umpteenth time, always just passing through – the reservation might as well have been a thousand miles away. I fishtailed out of the town of Garrison, leaving the lakeshore. I took highway 18 due west for a few miles. Everything was watery and green and depressing. I turned off and headed north again on highway 6, just a few miles more. Each road got a little bit narrower, the last being a one lane gravel driveway through a pioneer gate built with tamarack poles I peeled myself one crummy summer years ago when the Old Man was dying to get his mini-ranch started...

He wandered the property for weeks with a hundred foot tape and me on the short end, "Stand right there and don't move – got it?" I never bothered to answer. I knew when to stand still. He drove stakes in the ground and tied on little orange ribbons so they wouldn't get lost in the gray gray gray. He studied them for weeks, making little adjustments according to the angle of the sun, the position of the sandy garden, the crabapple trees, the horseshoe pit. He bought a six month lease on fifty acres of Tamarack swamp, so we could harvest the post and poles for the corral, gate and fence.

Come winter, when the swamp froze over and it was cold as hell, the Old Man dragged Big Sister and I out there on the back of his Allis Chalmers tractor, twenty-some-odd miles. Big Sister sat on a fender while I balanced on the trailer hitch. One slip and I was a goner. I clung for life to the back of the Old Man's grease stained jacket. I arrived on burning feet, tingling from the frozen heat and the rattling tractor. We trekked behind the Old Man, through waist high snow, to the middle of the fifty acre Tamarack swamp and he went to work with his chainsaw, taking down every tamarack tree he deemed reasonably fit for a fence. He brought down and cut up short fat ones for posts and long skinny ones for poles. He set Big Sister and I to knocking off the little branches with a stick and clearing away the things he deemed necessary for his sanity. He'd scream and swing the chainsaw at us, attempting to communicate his needs, wishes, demands.

For lunch we built a tamarack twig fire and boiled coffee and roasted hotdogs on the end of one of the spiny sticks we had beaten into the snow. After several weekends of this, the Old Man got Junkyard King to bring his big boom truck and we snaked the logs out of there to the side of the road with the Allis Chalmers. Junkyard King lifted them over the side with a metal claw, trucked them to the Old Man's mini ranch and dumped them in a pile out back.

The Old Man negotiated the terms of my contract for peeling the bark off the posts and the poles the following summer. He concluded that a nickel a post and a dime a pole would be sufficient. He bought a draw knife to accomplish the task and said it was mine for life, so charged me full price, including tax. I was already more than fifteen dollars in the hole. The day after school let out for summer vacation, the Old Man kicked over a couple fifty gallon drums and lined them up on the ground like saw horses then told me to pickup a pole and set it on them, grab the drawknife, straddle the pole and have at her. Less than a dozen passes with the drawknife, the blade was dull and caked with sap. I tried to brush it off, sideways, on the edge of the fifty gallon drums. As for all the gnarly knots, I employed a hatchet on the big ones and got out my frustrations on them. I chopped them to pieces, got struck in the eye by flying sappy chunks of Tamarack, nearly swung the hatchet into a thigh a couple times before settling back down to the drawknife. The Tamarack sap clogged my open pores then, dried in a jealous rage. I was married to it, couldn't scrub it off with the Lava soap. It stayed stuck to my hair and skin all summer, peaking in mid August when the milkweed and monarch butterflies and chokecherries and muggy ninety degree heat rubbed up against my greasy cheeks.

Come September, the day before school was to begin again, I finished. I threw away my sappy jeans and drawknife and hatchet and figured out in my head that I had at least a couple hundred dollars coming to me. I approached the Old Man regarding the fulfillment of the contract. His mood had shifted and, besides, he didn't like the puff in my chest, "Goddamn it kid, don't I do enough for you around here? You're eating right, you've got a bed to sleep on. You've got it good! Besides, you did a piss poor job of it." I couldn't deny that...

I spent my last days hanging around the Northland. The wolf was gone. I was a lingering ghost absorbing one last time whatever there was in the air or on the ground – the stick thin trees – the starving corn – the emptiness. Empty like me. Anyway, once I left I knew I wouldn't be coming back and that made it difficult to leave. Luckily, everyone kept reminding me of my wordy intentions muttered the previous Christmas, "I'm getting the fuck out of this place – see you fuckers later – ha ha ha – you, you, you, shitless wonders."

They laughed and laughed, "Your going-away party was three months ago. You're full of shit like always. You're gonna hang around here forever."

Last Verse

I hooked up the trailer and filled it with all my leftover crap: old motorcycle, weight set, broken guitar, Sears toolkit, box of books, memories. I threw a cheap tarp over the top and tied it down with my nylon hope – it practically blew off the first mile. I pulled over and made some adjustments, then, repeated that pattern so many times I gave up and the tarp gathered itself in the far corner.

Everything disappeared somewhere along the road. My memories were the first to go, in the Dakotas. The Sears toolkit was next, looted by some cowboy pirates on the Eastern Montana plain. I blew the engine in the Bitterroot mountains and was swindled out of the motorcycle and weight set for a tow and gimpy replacement. I lost the last box near Coeur d'Alene, sweaters the Mom had knitted and given every Christmas like a Salvation Army donation. The older ones were misshapen from when she was still working out the bones of it. The newer ones were nearly perfect, you could see the art of commitment. As each item disappeared from the wagon, my happiness increased.

I pulled into every truck stop along the way just for the hell of it – one more spoonful of gravy and bona fides – the crooked teeth the cheesy complexions – what a wonderful horrible mess. I crawled through the parking lots and took big whiffs of the diesel-gas-meat-potato breeze. I drifted off the freeway and wound along old state routes and back roads. I had plenty of time to consider things – whatever things – ridiculous things – bottomless things – starry things.

I rolled into the state of Washington with an empty wagon, free for the first time in my entire life – it felt great – wiped clean – no chance for a corporate career, or politics, ethics, law, management. I was free of America and America was free of me. I took the long climb out of Spokane – drove on a lava bed millions of years old through wheat fields on the northwest desert plateau – a joy ride to the bottom of the gorge over the Columbia river, then, an old car horrifying death climb up the other side – better turn off the air conditioning – get out and run along side – pull over and rest – take it in strides.

A thin evergreen forest appeared, then got thicker and thicker – green layered on green layered on green – every shade – it was overwhelming – the aching green – the dirty green – the pungent green – the green green green.

I drove through Snoqualmie Pass and rock walls covered with rivulets of water, tiny escape routes for the run off – as steep as they could take it – ocean bound – like me – finally – running toward something instead of running away, always running away. There was a good side back there somewhere, it was just so damn hard to remember. Nothing to do but push forward and carry along a little ember.

I dropped out of the Cascades doing ninety. My empty wagon pushed me along with its desire to be refilled. Never again. Still, my empty wagon knew something – something I couldn't scrape off the bottom of my shoe – it stayed straight while I swerved in front.

My car had enough broken parts dangling in the slipstream to ward off all evil spirits of the road, with their twisted necks and branded eyes, they blurred backwards through the evergreen background in their newer better rides. I let out a, "Whaa-hooooo!" for old time's sake and left them to wallow in my dirty blue exhaust. My momentum took me over eastern suburban tracks running up the hillsides – they smelled of oil and gas. I drove on a floating bridge toward a ferry terminal. Traffic stopped dead on the bridge. The radiator cooling fan was busted, so when the car wasn't moving, the temperature gauge shot right up into the red and steam rose from the radiator cap. I counted the quicksand minutes in the inch-along traffic. Everybody was going the same direction as I. At mid bridge the car died a burning boiling death. I got out and popped the hood and looked under like I meant to address the issue, but I knew, when the steamy white turned to smoky blue, that it would be over soon and I'd be back on my feet. I dropped the hood and grabbed the plastic garbage bag from behind the seat and walked away from the traffic jam, snickering like the devil.

It was one last little thing. I was going to soak in the Sound and see what happened to the wolf – the appetite – the sorrow – the smart ass – the thief – the drunk – the dreamer – the loser – the talker – the dickhead – the pleaser – the Big Dipper – the end.

Made in the USA
Charleston, SC
10 January 2012